HIS PROPOSAL

BY

ANGEL RAYNE

Published by Everblood Publishing, LLC
https://everbloodpublishing.com

ISBN-13: 978-1-945499-75-3

Cover Design by Coffee and Characters

Proofreader: Mackenzie @ NiceGirlNaughtyEdits.com

ALSO BY ANGEL RAYNE

Mafia Romance Reading Order

Luca and Veda

His Game

His Stakes

His Win

Enzo and Sera

His Promise

His Rejection

His Proposal

Stand Alone Novels

Tyler and Ailee

Be With Me

SYNOPSIS

I may be a monster, but I always get what I want.

Letting Serafina go was a mistake. Maybe the biggest I've ever made.

Too bad I didn't realize it until she was forced into an arranged marriage with my worst enemy.

I've always done whatever the mafia asked of me. Gave up everything I loved in the process.

But I won't do it this time.

Because even though she hates me for betraying her, I'll make her love me again—even if I have to wage a brutal war in her name. Hell, I'll burn my life to the ground and let her bathe in the ashes if that's what she wants.

In the end, Sera will be my wife.

And God have mercy on our enemies, because I sure as hell won't...

CHAPTER 1

Enzo

Luca's voice, low and urgent, filtered through the fog of rage that blocked out everything and everyone other than the woman standing in front of the altar. He grabbed the front of my shirt, and slowly, the red haze on the outskirts of my vision shifted.

"Enzo. Listen to me. You cannot react." I tried to look around him, but he wouldn't allow it. "This is what he wants. He's using her to get to you, hoping you'll start something. I know what you're feeling. Trust me, I do. But if you do anything right now except sit back down in that fucking pew, it will give him the excuse he needs to take me out. To take *all* of us out. So sit the fuck down. We can't win this, my friend. Not today."

What he was saying finally infiltrated, and I blinked as his pale face came into focus, his blue eyes wide and locked on mine through the lenses of my sunglasses as he tried to get through to me.

"Sit. The. Fuck. Down," he ordered. "Do *not* make a scene."

I wanted to obey him. I've always obeyed him, ever since he rose to the position of underboss and Tristan and I vowed it with blood and honor. But I couldn't think. Couldn't move.

A soft hand took mine.

"Enzo."

I looked down to see Veda's hand gripping mine, and then my eyes rose to her face. She was scared. I didn't like it when she was scared.

"Please," she whispered.

The music had stopped. We were the only ones left standing. Abruptly, I took my seat, still holding Veda's hand to anchor me to the spot. With a sigh of relief, Luca sat down on her other side. Tristan said something to him and he shook his head, then smiled at Veda and took her other hand before giving his attention to the people standing at the front of the church.

I stared straight ahead as the priest began the ceremony. I couldn't look at Luigi's new bride. Couldn't watch as she agreed to spend the rest of her life with a man who was old enough to be her father. Or grandfather, even. A man who had ordered me to kill my wife without an ounce of emotion.

And I had. I'd done it. To prove my loyalty to him and his son. A loyalty he didn't deserve.

I felt Luigi's eyes on me. He was fucking enjoying this. He expected me to make a scene, perhaps threaten his life, just as Luca said. As a matter of fact, I'd bet he was counting on it.

But I wouldn't give him the fucking satisfaction. So I sat my ass in the pew and showed nothing of what I was feeling, even as I burned alive from the inside out, the back of my neck prickling from the curious eyes of many of the guests wondering what the fuck was going on. But I refused to show any reaction to the fact that the woman who haunted my every waking moment and possessed my dreams was marrying a man I hated.

Inside, however, I was screaming.

As the ceremony dragged out, the roar in my head grew louder until I could only hope my memories of this day would become nothing but one big blur. However, that wasn't the case. For I would remember every specific detail, each one like a razor blade cutting into my skin over and over and over again. The priest droning on and on. The restless movements of the guests. And the murmured responses of the man and woman standing in front of the altar.

At one point, I must've moved or made some sound, for I saw Luca lean over Veda in my peripheral.

"Keep it together, Enz."

I glanced over at him and then down at my hands fisted in my lap. Slowly, I relaxed them.

Sera's shaky voice penetrated my violent thoughts. "I, Serafina Cordaro, take you...Luigi Morelli, for my lawful husband. To have and to...hold...from this day forward... for better, for worse...for richer, for poorer, in sickness and in health..." Her voice tapered off, and I couldn't stop myself from finding her, standing there looking so fucking beautiful she burned my eyes and made my heart skip.

"...until death do us part," she finally finished.

The buzzing began in my ears and slowly spread throughout my body until I was physically shaking with the need to pull out my gun and shoot the man standing in front of her. Only Veda's hand on my arm stopped me from doing it. If I shot Luigi here, in front of so many of his friends, the entire place would erupt into gunfire. Sera could be harmed. Or Veda. Or any of the other innocent women or children in the church.

I couldn't be the cause of such a slaughter. Not again.

So I tore my eyes away from her and kept my ass on that hard, wooden pew, stewing in my rage and disbelief as this hoax of a ceremony went on, and I stared at the statue in front of me until the scar below my left eye throbbed painfully with every beat of my heart. The scar from the bullet I'd taken.

For her.

To save *her*.

The crowded church erupted into cheers as Luca's father put his slimy mouth on my Sera's sweet lips. Lucky for him, he kept it short and sweet, or I wouldn't have been able to control my reaction no matter what the consequences. By the time the music started again and the newly married bride and groom turned to face their guests before making their way back down the aisle together, every muscle in my body ached from holding myself so still in the pew.

I jumped out of my seat and crossed in front of my friends, shaking off the hands that tried to stop me. I stood at the head of the aisle, watching the woman I wanted more than anything in this life walk away from me as another man's wife.

I could shoot him right now in the back of the head. Easily. All I had to do was pull out my gun and aim.

Before I realized what I was doing, my hand was sliding inside my jacket.

The couple paused halfway down the aisle to receive congratulations. Sera stopped when Luigi did, turning her profile to me, and I saw the corner of her mouth lift into a timid smile. As though she felt me there, watching her, she looked back over her shoulder and her eyes searched for mine. They dropped down to my hand inside of my jacket, and then back up to my face. Was that a flash of hope on her perfect face? Looking away from me, she smiled again and then placed her hand inside Luigi's elbow and continued down the aisle.

Slowly, I dropped my arm back onto my side. When I turned, I found Luca watching me, waiting to see what I would do, but not trying to stop me this time. We stared at each other for a long moment, and then I took a step back and allowed my friends to walk ahead of me as we followed the other guests out of the church.

No one spoke until we were inside our vehicle with the doors closed. Tristan was driving. My hands were shaking too hard to grip the wheel.

Luca spoke from the backseat. "We need to go to the reception, and you need to be there, Enzo."

"No." I couldn't do it. I'd barely survived the ceremony.

"This is a game," Luca said. "You know it as well as I."

He was right. I did know. I knew exactly why he had married her. "He thinks we won't come for him if he has Sera."

"Exactly." Luca paused. "And he's right. If I go after him now, she will also be in danger. And not just from me, but from anyone who covets my father's position as boss."

"I don't understand," Veda said.

"There are only two ways my father will give up his position within the family. By stepping down gracefully, which we know he will not do, or if he's dead."

"You plan to kill him," Veda said, her voice soft and incredulous.

"Yes," Luca told her honestly. "That was always the plan."

I didn't have to look at her to see the horrified expression in her eyes. Veda wasn't from the world of the mafia. She didn't understand the way it worked. And sometimes, I wondered if she would survive staying with Luca. But their relationship wasn't mine to worry about. "I can*not* go there," I told him.

"You must," Luca ordered.

I threw my head back against the headrest. "Jesus fucking Christ." My lungs felt tight. I couldn't breathe. I needed to get out of this fucking car. "Let me out," I told Tristan.

"Enzo, what are you doing?" Luca asked.

"Stop the fucking car and let me OUT!"

Tristan glanced over at me and then pulled the SUV onto the side of the road. My seatbelt was off and I was out of the vehicle before it had even fully stopped. I felt like I was going to vomit.

"You didn't want her, remember? You gave her back to her father. What the hell did you think was going to happen?"

Yanking my sunglasses off, I wiped the sweat out of my eyes. "Get the fuck away from me, Luca."

He walked around in front of me, one hand shoving my shoulder so hard my back slammed into the side of the SUV. "Get it fucking together," he growled in my face. "This is what you wanted. We are going to the fucking reception, and you are going to be there with me."

"I didn't want *this*," I hissed at him.

He paced away from me, hands on his hips as he struggled to control his temper. When he did, he turned back to me. "I need you there, Enzo."

I shook my head. "I can't, Luca. I can't. You can't ask this of me."

His large hands cupped the sides of my head, forcing me to look at him. What he saw in my eyes made the remaining anger drain from his own. "You know I wouldn't ask this of you if I didn't have to," he said. "But if we let him win this battle, it will ruin everything that we've accomplished up until now. Everyone will think I'm a fucking coward. They will think *you* are a fucking coward. Everyone we've brought to our side will turn against us in a heartbeat. You know this as well as I do. And we've worked too fucking hard to let that happen. What will happen to us, to Veda—to *Sera*—if my father stays in power? What do you think he will do to her?"

I swallowed hard, and knocked his hands away.

But he wasn't about to let me go that easily. "We need to show up, and I need you to find that place inside of you that feels nothing. I need you to go there, and stay there. We will toast to the bride and groom, I will dance with Veda, we will eat the expensive fucking food, and you will show my father that you don't care. And then, when we are ready, I will deal with my father. But not before we are ready, or it will be a death sentence for all of us."

"And what about Sera?"

Luca glanced over my shoulder to where Veda remained in the car waiting for him, and I knew he was trying to put himself in my shoes. "She's strong, and she knows what's expected of her. She will survive until we can get her." Luca reached for my shoulder and placed a comforting hand there. "It won't be long now. I should have enough of the family on my side within a few weeks. She'll be okay until then."

That may be true, but I didn't know if I would be.

"We have to do this, Enzo."

I closed my eyes and breathed in through my nose, trying to find that place he spoke of. It used to be more easily accessible. After another few minutes, I nodded, and hid the last of my emotions behind my sunglasses.

We got back into the SUV, and Tristan took us to the reception.

CHAPTER 2

Serafina

A few weeks earlier...

I watched Enzo walk into the elevator, my entire body numb with disbelief.

He was leaving me.

He was fucking leaving me.

How was this possible? My mind couldn't correlate this man with the man I'd gotten to know these last weeks. The one who'd offered me an obscene amount of money just to fuck me. Who'd hunted down the bastard who'd sold me to human traffickers. The man who'd then stolen me back, killing everyone who got in his way. The man who'd lost his mind when I'd tried to leave him. I could not equate that man with *this* man who had just coldheartedly turned me back over to my father. The one person in the world I was trying to escape.

Luca was talking. Saying something to my father, then to me. But I couldn't hear him through the roar of blood rushing through my head.

The next thing I knew, my father was throwing his arms in the air, spittle flying from his mouth, and then two of my father's men appeared on either side of me. They took ahold of my arms, and in a daze, I stumbled along between them as they walked me into the elevator.

I was shoved into the back corner and nearly fell on my face when the heel of one of my shoes caught on the edge of the elevator floor, but I instinctively threw up my hands to steady myself on the back wall just in time. Yet, the world still tilted around me as I turned to face the doors. Between the shoulders of my father's men who stood in front of me blocking my way out, my eyes clashed with Luca's: hurt and disbelief in mine, anger and worry in his.

The doors began to slide closed and I blinked, waking up from the trance-like state that had held me immobile up until now. I lunged for the opening in a fit of panic and saw Luca take a step forward before he remembered himself and stopped. I was caught and held roughly. "Nooo!" I screamed as the doors slid shut.

A hand covered in rings flew toward my face, and then I remembered nothing else until I woke up on a private plane just as it hit the tarmac in Dallas.

"WHAT DO you have to say for yourself, Fina?"

I was in my room. The one I'd walked out of months ago and swore I would never see again. We'd just arrived from the airport, and my father had had his two goons escort me up here. I turned around slowly, seeing my four-poster bed with the white comforter covered in giant pink watercolor flowers, the walk-in closet still full of the clothes I'd left, the large white dresser, the small white desk and chair where I would sit and do my homework when I was in school, and the hope chest at the foot of the bed that held nothing but some extra blankets because nothing in this house was private. "Don't call me that."

"What did you say to me?"

Anger rose up inside of me as I turned to face my father. "I said not to call me that. I hate that name."

His neck and jowls flushed red. "It's your father's name for you. Are you telling me that you hate your father? That you hate me? The man who raised you? Who tried to protect you and keep you safe?"

"You kept me a prisoner."

He stepped closer to me, but I refused to be cowed. Not this time. "Of course, I did. I did what I had to do, Fina." His eyes swept over me, seeing past the pretty dress to the woman underneath. "Look at what happened as soon as you leave my house."

"And what is that?" I asked him.

His mouth twisted in disgust. "You became a whore. Just like your mother."

"Maybe if you'd kept her happy, she wouldn't have had to find it somewhere else."

A loud smack reverberated through the room. The sound hit my ears before I felt the pain. It started in my jaw before traveling up to my temple.

"You will remember who you are speaking to," he hissed.

Even with the physical reminder he'd just given me, it was surreal to me that I was back in this place. I hadn't been gone very long in the grand scheme of things, and yet it felt like those years I'd spent living in this house—in this room—were a lifetime ago. Maybe because I'd worked so hard to forget them.

I worked my jaw to make sure it wasn't broken. It hurt, but everything appeared to be in working order.

This was bullshit.

I didn't have to stay here.

Fuck these men and their over-inflated egos. They didn't have the right to tell me how I was going to live my life.

Without looking at my father, I started walking toward the bedroom door.

"Where do you think you're going?" he shouted after me.

I didn't bother to answer him. I wasn't going to stand here and argue about whether or not I had the right to decide what I was going to do with my own life.

"Fina! I'm talking to you!"

Reaching the door my father had slammed closed when we arrived, I turned the knob and yanked it open. I didn't try to bring anything with me. There was nothing I wanted that would remind me of this life. I also didn't have a car this time, and it wouldn't be so easy to get through the gates. I'm sure my father had all of the guards on alert. But none of that stopped me. I had to get out of there.

The two men who'd pulled me out of the room above Luca's club appeared in front of me, blocking my way. I tried to duck around one of them, but he grabbed me by the shoulders and shoved me hard, sending me stumbling back into the room. As if they were one person, they stepped over the threshold and blocked the only exit.

I spun around and faced my father. "You can't keep me here against my will."

But he just laughed. "Yes. I can."

"I'm a grown woman! I'm capable of making my own decisions for my life!"

"You are my daughter!" he yelled. "And you will do what I fucking tell you!" He stalked toward me, lowering his voice. And somehow that was more frightening than when he yelled. "And I'm telling you that you will stay here. You're a pretty woman, Fina. There are men who will still want you, despite the fact that you're used goods now."

"But what if I don't want them?"

"You will do what you have to do for the good of the family, and you'll be fucking grateful. Do you understand me?"

"I'm not worth anything to you anymore!" I shouted, my temper getting the best of me. "And I don't give a shit about you or this fucking family!" I tensed, waiting for the slap that was sure to come after that outburst. But it never did. Not from my father.

One thick hand reached up and grabbed the back of my hair, pulling it from its twist. He pulled until I was bent over backward and he was leaning over me. "You ungrateful bitch."

I glared up at him. Let him kill me now. I was done sitting here meekly while he pawned me off like a piece of property rather than a child of his own flesh and blood.

After a moment, he released me, and I fell to the floor. He stepped over me like I was nothing but a piece of trash. "Do what you need to do to get her in line," he told his men. "But she is not to be raped and she is not to leave this room. She might still be worth something."

Scrambling up from the floor, I shoved my hair from my face and stared at them with a defiant expression.

The guard to my right smiled as he cracked the knuckles of his right hand, and my heart stuttered in my chest.

"Serafina!"

I jumped, hot tea sloshing over the cup I held and burning my fingers. Quickly, I set it down on the table before I dropped it and angered him more.

"Did you hear me?"

"Yes," I told him.

"I can't hear you."

I lifted my chin. My father sat across from me in the kitchen, a cloth napkin tucked into the front of his shirt and a knife and fork in his hands, paused over the steak he'd been cutting as he'd casually told me that he'd found me a husband.

My hands began to shake and I tucked them under my legs, the rough material of the jeans I wore scraping painfully against the new burns. "Yes," I told him, louder this time. "I heard you."

His dark eyes studied my face, searching for any hint of rebellion. But that had been beaten out of me days ago. I was still sporting the bruises. And today was the first day I'd been allowed to leave my room. "Aren't you happy? Now you can finally start your life. Have a family."

I didn't ask who the lucky guy was. I was afraid to know.

"He's even overlooking the fact that you're a whore. Isn't that good of him?" He smiled at me, as if he hadn't just called his only daughter a derogatory word, and shoved a large piece of steak into his mouth, chewing loudly before he swallowed and slurped his wine. "Maybe you'll even make me a *nonno*. It would be nice to have some little faces running around."

My stomach lurched at the thought of giving him more children to torture. *My* children.

He waved his knife in the air. "You'll need to do something with that hair. I can have a stylist come to the house."

"I like my hair," I told him. And then I froze, half expecting that knife to come flying at my face. The protest had just come out before I thought about what I was saying.

But to my surprise, he only shrugged. "Keep it then. Let your new husband deal with you. I'm tired of fighting."

The air left my lungs in a rush and spots danced in front of my eyes. I gripped my chair tight, willing myself not to fall out of it. I hadn't eaten much in the last few days. My stomach tied itself in knots every time my mind replayed Enzo walking away from me. The last thing he'd said constantly ringing in my ears.

"I will not be forced into marrying your daughter. Go ahead and take her if you think you can get anything for her."

And then, he'd walked away. As though my lack of innocence disgusted him, when he was the one who'd stolen it.

"How much are you getting?" I asked.

My father shook his head, his eyes on his dinner. "That's not your business, Fina."

I almost laughed, but I caught myself just in time.

"Aren't you going to ask me about your fiancé´?"

No. I was too afraid.

But my father kept talking, as if I wasn't sitting here with this look of terror on my face.

"You know Luigi Morelli?"

My blood cooled as the name registered, gradually turning to ice.

"He's the boss down in Austin. I'm sure you've heard of him."

Yes. I knew who he was very well.

"I thought since you liked it there so much that you would like to go back. Make a real home there with your new husband."

My hand shook as I picked up my tea. "In other words, you want me to spy for you."

He looked up from his dinner, an expression of denial on his face. "No, of course not! I would never ask you to betray your new husband. Why would you say such a thing?"

It would've almost been convincing if it wasn't for the calculated look in his eyes.

When I didn't respond, he shrugged. "But perhaps if you happened to innocently overhear any useful information, you might casually mention it when you speak to me."

Except there was only one flaw in his plan. Once I was out of here, I planned to never speak to him again.

I may be beaten, but I was not broken.

"You will be married on Christmas Eve," my father droned on. "I chose that date because I know how much you love Christmas." He set down his knife and fork. "What do you say to me, Fina?"

I set my cup down carefully, and tried to speak past the lump in my throat. "Thank you."

Satisfied, my father went back to his meal. I stared down into my tea, my mind blank and my body numb. Later, when I was alone in my room, I would cry. But not now. Not in front of him.

Never in front of him.

CHAPTER 3

Enzo

Current Day

The reception was being held at a hotel not far from the church. When we walked in, we were informed by the concierge that the entire sixth floor had been reserved for those who wished to stay the night at the expense of the groom.

Tristan and I hung back as Luca and Veda walked over to the newly married couple and gave them their congratulations. Only those who knew him very well would notice the tense set of Luca's shoulders, or the way his smile did not quite reach his eyes.

And only someone who was standing directly behind them would see the way his hand gripped the back of

Veda's dress, as though he were afraid someone would try to take her from him. Which wasn't as crazy as it sounded.

As Luca had ordered, and for the safety of everyone there, I hid my pain behind the dark lenses of my sunglasses and the relaxed, yet alert, posture of my body. If anyone who had been at the wedding was curious as to my reaction to the bride, they didn't dare say anything to me about it. I kept my eyes averted from Sera, because if I looked at her, if I saw the trapped expression on her face, there was no way in hell I'd be able to leave her here. With him.

But even though on the outside I held myself completely in check, I couldn't do what Luca had asked. I couldn't shut myself down. Not completely. What had once been so easy for me was now impossible.

And it was all because of her.

We lingered in the reception area only as long as absolutely necessary, and then we headed inside to eat and drink and act like none of this was as fucked up as it actually was. Luckily, the fact that I was on duty saved me from having to partake with the other guests, because there was no way in hell I would've been able to choke anything down. Not when my guts twisted and my head pounded as I watch the woman who was mine sit beside her new husband.

I'd never hated him as much as I did in this moment. Not even when the son of a bitch had ordered me to shoot my own wife. No, that wasn't true. I did hate him then. I just didn't allow myself to feel it. I was a soldier before I was anything else, and I did what I was ordered to do. No questions asked. Not even if they were burning inside of me.

I stood behind Luca and Veda as they ate and drank and danced, and this time I could no longer keep my eyes from straying toward the woman seated at the front of the room. Her face frozen in a mask of acceptance, she wouldn't return my attention. But I noticed that even though she had her wineglass refilled often, she barely ate anything. And when Luigi took her out onto the dance floor for the first dance of the bride and groom, she was stiff and uncoordinated.

At one point, I saw her wince when her new husband squeezed her hand too tight. I took a step forward, my only thought to remove his fucking touch from her, but Tristan's hand shot out to grip my arm, stopping me. My jaw clenched so hard it made my teeth ache, I took a step back, taking my place beside him once more. In my peripheral, I saw her father, Ciro, watching me carefully from his table near the bride and groom's.

Taking a calming breath, I clasped my hands in front of me and went back to watching for any threats to my boss.

When the first dance as husband and wife was over, Sera immediately removed herself from the circle of his arms.

But Luigi wasn't finished with her yet, and he took her hand and led her over to a table of mafia men and their wives so he could show her off. After introductions were made, she leaned into him and spoke into his ear. He shook his head, and she tried again, more urgently this time. After giving her a threatening look and what I could only imagine were words of warning, Luigi snapped his fingers at one of his guards and let her go. Quickly, she crossed the floor and headed toward the double doors that led out into the hall, the guard close on her heels.

I watched her go until she was out of sight and Luigi had turned back to his friends. Then I glanced toward Ciro. He was standing up, his back to us as he chuckled about something with one of the other guests. "I'll be right back," I told Tristan.

His eyes never leaving the crowd he scanned, he asked, "Enzo, what are you doing?"

"I'll be right back," I repeated. As discreetly as possible, I followed her across the floor. By the time I got out of the room and into the hall, she was nowhere to be found. Following my instincts, I turned left and headed toward the restrooms.

As I rounded the corner, I saw Luigi's guard standing outside the ladies' room. My steps were silent on the carpeted floor as I approached. He didn't so much as glance up from his phone until I was right on top of him. Without a word, I shoved him up against the wall with my hands around his throat. I squeezed until his eyes rolled back into his head and his legs gave out.

His body slid down the wall as he passed out cold. After a quick look up and down the hallway, I grabbed him by the shoulders of his jacket and dragged him into the men's room. Luckily, it was empty, and I sat him up in the stall. By the time he woke up and realized what had happened, we would be long gone.

Sera was standing in front of the gold-rimmed mirror when I barged into the ladies' room without announcing my presence. Her eyes flashed to my face, and for an instant, I thought I saw relief in the blue-gray depths. But it was there and gone so fast that I questioned whether I'd ever really seen it at all.

"Get out," she told me.

"Sera…"

"I said. Get. Out."

"No."

I stalked toward her as she backed away, throwing one hand up, as if that would stop me. She made to run around me out the door, but I anticipated that she would do exactly that and I lunged to the side, lifting her up off her feet and into my arms. Through the overpowering scent of the bouquets of roses that decorated the sink, I caught a whiff of coconuts and tropical flowers that made my heart ache inside my chest.

Bold as you please, she stared up at me, her eyes dull and cold. A direct contrast to her scent that warmed my soul. "I'll scream," she threatened, but I had a hard time believing she would. I was greatly outnumbered here, with only Luca and Tristan and perhaps a small handful of others to back me up. If she carried through with that threat, the odds of walking out of here alive weren't great.

I cocked my head to the side. "Do you want me dead?"

Her upper lip twisted into a sneer. "Why should I care what happens to you? What do you want, Enzo?"

I couldn't answer her, because I didn't know. Not exactly. I just knew I had to see her to see if...what? If she hated me? If she still wanted me?

When I still didn't release her, she shoved at my chest. "Get off of me. Let me go."

Her protests didn't faze me. After what I'd done to her, I expected her to be angry. But what tore a fucking hole in my chest was the complete and utter lack of emotion in her eyes and voice as she tried to get me to release her.

Words hung on the tip of my tongue. Things I needed to say. But after her initial struggle, she turned her face to the side and just...waited. I stilled as a cold shiver traveled down my spine. But then I got angry. I was not some fucking green boy she could just ignore and I would go away.

Opening my arms, I released her so fast she would've fallen backwards if I hadn't caught her. Her hair was down except for a diamond clasp on the crown of her head holding some of it off her face. I fisted the silky pink strands in one hand and forced her head back. She grunted with pain and closed her eyes, her lips pressed tightly together.

That wasn't going to fucking work for me.

Grabbing her jaw, I pressed my fingers and thumb into her cheeks between her teeth until she opened for me, and then I took her mouth, kissing her with all the self-loathing and frustration inside of me. She tasted sweet, like wine, and I moaned, fucking her mouth with my tongue the way I wished I could fuck her body, unable to get enough of this woman I wouldn't let myself have.

I was so hungry for her that it took me a minute to realize she wasn't responding to me the way I was to her. Frustration ripped through me, and I sank my teeth into her bottom lip until I tasted the salty copper of her blood, trying to force a reaction from her. I didn't give a shit what kind of emotion it was. I just needed something, anything, that would let me know she was still in there. Somewhere. That my rejection hadn't completely destroyed the girl she was.

Hadn't completely destroyed *us*.

But other than a hiss of pain, there was nothing. She didn't even try to push me away again. She just hung there in my arms, limp, like some kind of drugged-up rag doll.

Wrapping my hand around her throat, I shoved my face down into hers. "Stop pretending you don't feel anything. Because I know you fucking do."

"That's where you're wrong," she rasped, and I realized I was squeezing a little too hard. I loosened my fingers just a bit. Slowly, she opened her eyes...

...and my heart stopped. They were dead. Emotionless. My skin broke out in gooseflesh as she told me in that same flat tone, "I did. Once. Feel something for you. But now I know how little I mean to you. So, you want to fuck me one last time? Is that what you want, Enzo? Then do it and get it over with. My husband is waiting for me."

Each word sliced through my skin with the pain of a dull knife. "You're lying."

"I'm not," she insisted. "And when I go back in there, I'll tell him that you raped me. Just like you did that night in front of your guards." Disgust twisted her mouth. "I guess I should be grateful there're no witnesses this time."

I stared down into her unblinking eyes, searching for the light that once sparkled within them. The light that lit up my darkness and made me crave things I had no business wanting. But there was nothing. Not even a glimmer.

Roughly, I shoved her away from me. And I was glad that I hadn't taken off my sunglasses and let her see how she tore me up inside. "I will not apologize for being a monster. After all, no one has ever told me they were sorry for making me this way. I am the way I am so I could survive. And that is exactly what I've done." I let my eyes roam over her face one more time. "Have a good life, Sera."

Turning on my heel, I left her standing there in the empty restroom, surrounded by white tiles as cold as she was.

CHAPTER 4

Serafina

After he left, I stood frozen for a long time, afraid to move for fear I would break into a million tiny pieces. But I couldn't stop the tears from silently tracking down my cheeks. Or the way my hands shook when I finally reached for a tissue out of the box in the middle of the sink.

My eye makeup was running down my face, revealing streaks of the purplish bruise that darkened the skin below my left eye. A parting gift from my father when I'd tried one last time to talk him out of this farce of a marriage. Tired of my arguing with him, he'd hauled back and slammed his fist into my face. I'd fallen into the chair behind me, my father's home office fading in and out of the edges of my vision.

"What is this, Fina? Hmm? Why can you not appreciate what I've done for you?" he'd asked me. Then he bent down over me where I sat sprawled out in the chair, pain ricocheting through my eye socket and cheekbone. "The daughter I knew before you ran off would never have been so ungrateful."

I'd glared up at him. "What exactly do I have to be grateful for? That you forced me back into a life I hate? And are now forcing me into a marriage I will hate even more?"

"This life you hate so much kept you in clothes with a roof over your head and food on your table. It paid for you to go to college—"

"It made me a prisoner!" I'd yelled into his face, then I'd squeezed my eyes shut and thrown up my hands, bracing myself for another hit, but it never came.

Instead, my father had just smirked down at me, then straightened to his full height. "I told you, I'm finished fighting with you, Fina. Let your new husband have that pleasure." A smile had broken out onto his face. "I told him you were a feisty one! He's looking forward to breaking you in." Walking back around his desk, he'd sat down and started shuffling through the papers waiting for his attention. "Go clean yourself up and get some sleep. You're getting married tomorrow."

After a moment, I'd sat up and gingerly touched my eye and checked my nose ring to make sure it hadn't gotten ripped out of my nose.

"Out, Fina," my father had ordered.

Shaking off the memory, I used the tissue to try to blend the layers of foundation the makeup artist had used to cover the discoloration, but mostly, the only thing I succeeded in doing was to rub more of it off. At least she'd used waterproof mascara, so I didn't have black streaks running down my cheeks.

I blotted the last of the tear stains away as best I could and then checked my dress. It was a gorgeous traditional number with cap sleeves, a modest neckline, lots of sequins, big skirts, and completely inappropriate for this time of year. It was also not my style at all. But it was what my father could find within his budget on short notice.

The ring on my finger flashed in the mirror, reflecting the light, and I froze. It suddenly hit me. I was now Luigi Morelli's wife. When I left this fancy party, it would be with him. When I went to bed tonight, it would be with him. When I woke up tomorrow, it would be with him.

And whatever happened during the night, it would be with him.

Suddenly, I couldn't get enough air in my lungs. I pulled at the neckline of my dress, tearing the delicate fabric, desperate for breath. Except for my minor outburst the night before, I'd been walking through the last few days as if I were someone else watching another woman's life unfold before my eyes. And only now was the reality of my situation really hitting me.

I was a mafia bride. Sold to the highest bidder, just like I'd always feared. My life no longer my own. The property of the man who was now my husband. And he could do whatever the hell he wanted with me, and no one in this world would blink an eye.

For a moment, the image of Enzo standing with me in front of the altar flashed before my eyes, and I bent forward as the fist that had been squeezing my chest finally let go and sweet oxygen rushed into my lungs.

A dream. It was only a dream.

One that would never become real.

THE REMAINDER of the reception was a blur, and way too soon, I was in the back seat of a black Lincoln with my new husband. I still choked on the word whenever I said it, even if it was just in my head.

Two other cars traveled with us, one in front of us and one behind us. The guard in the front passenger seat and the one sitting beside me were both openly carrying a submachine gun. Something I knew was illegal, even in Texas.

Of course, the mafia made their own laws.

We pulled up to the house—made of stone and isolated like Luca's, but not as grand—and I was shown upstairs by a woman with brassy hair wearing a pound of makeup and dressed in an old-fashioned maid's outfit. She didn't speak, and neither did I as she took me to my new bedroom. As we walked through the door, any and all hope I had of having my own room flew out the window.

Lamps on either side of the large bed let off a soft, warm light. The red comforter on the bed was turned down. If the closet full of suits hadn't given it away, I would've known by the dark colors and large, bulky furniture that this was Luigi's room. It was your typical old-school mafia decor—all black and gold and red. The rest of the house, from what I'd seen of it as I was rushed upstairs, was decorated in a similar manner.

It reminded me a lot of my father's house, and my stomach twisted until I thought I was going to be sick.

I realized she was staring at me, waiting. "What?" I asked her. My tone was rude, but I didn't care. Although maybe I should. It would be nice to have at least one friend in this house. Instead of answering me, she gestured with one finger that I was to turn around. With a frown, I did as she asked, and felt her hands on the back of my dress as she began to unfasten the buttons that ran down my back.

Oh.

"But I have nothing to wear," I protested as I struggled to keep the front of my gown up even as she tried to tug it down.

"There's something for you in the closet," she snapped. "And what the hell does it matter? You're his *wife* now."

I got the distinct feeling that this woman was as happy about me being here as I was. Maybe that could work to my advantage. Letting my arms fall back down to my sides, I allowed her to tug the bodice of the dress off my shoulders until the whole thing dropped to the floor around my feet. I stepped out of it and waited, wearing only a one-piece, white shapewear thing that I was sure was going to leave permanent marks on my belly and hips and barely covered my breasts. I hated the damn thing, but there was no way I would've fit into the dress without it.

My eyes followed her as she took the wedding gown my father had spent a small fortune on over to the closet, balling it up in her arms none too gently, and I almost smiled as sequins popped off and skipped across the floor.

But the amusement fell from my face when she came back out with a black gossamer nightgown so sheer I wondered what the hell the point of wearing it was. "I'm not putting that on," I told her.

"Fine. Be naked." Dropping the thing on the red comforter of the bed, she walked behind me again and started unfastening the laces of the torture device that was holding everything in.

I tried to step away from her, but she followed me, hanging onto the laces, until I was pressed up against the wall beside the bathroom door. "Stop!" I yelled. "I'm not taking this off."

She heaved a harassed sigh. "You can let me help you take the damn thing off, or you can wait for Luigi to cut it off of you. And let me tell you, I know from experience that he has no regard for the skin underneath. So which is it gonna be?"

After a moment's contemplation, I stopped fighting her. She was right. What was the use? No one was coming to save me this time. Enzo wasn't going to come busting in here to carry me away from my nightmare. He'd gotten what he'd wanted from me and then given me back to my father without a backward glance, effectively getting out of his end of the deal we'd made. And it was time I faced the truth and stopped living in a fantasy world.

He didn't give a shit about me.

My reluctant assistant finally loosened the last lace and hook, and I sucked in a great lungful of air as the contraption released me from its grasp. I helped her push it over my hips and down my legs, one hand on the wall as I stepped out of it. Glancing down, I saw that I was right. Ugly red marks streaked my skin, some so dark I wondered if it was possible for shapewear to leave bruises.

"Put on the nightgown," she ordered. "Your...*husband*... will be in shortly."

I looked up just in time to see her marching out of the bedroom, her spine so stiff I wondered if she was also forced to wear uncomfortable underthings.

She slammed the door behind her, and I bent down to pick up the shapewear, tossing it into the closet on top of the wedding gown where she'd left it on the floor. My new friend didn't seem thrilled with the fact that there was another woman in the house, and I wondered what her relationship with Luigi was. Not that I cared. As far as I was concerned, she could have him.

I searched the closet for something else to wear. There was no way I was going to wear that thing on the bed if I could help it. That was something a woman wore when she wanted to seduce her new husband. Luigi may force me to have sex with him, but I sure as hell wasn't going to pretend that I wanted it to happen.

Finding nothing but suits and dress shirts, I rushed over to the dresser. I had no idea when Luigi would be joining me, and I didn't want him to walk in and catch me standing here naked. With that thought in mind, I went over to the bed and grabbed the nightgown and threw it over my head. It was sheer and sleeveless, with a low-cut neckline, but at least I felt like I had something on.

Back at the dresser, I found nothing but some tighty-whitey underwear and socks, along with a drawer full of ties and wrist cuffs. Shoving the door shut, I went back to the closet, searching for a robe...anything. I eyed the dress shirts. Luigi wasn't a large man, and I didn't think they'd cover anything, but I was getting desperate, so I tugged one off its hanger and stuck my arms through the sleeves. It barely covered my ass, and I couldn't button it across my chest, but at least it was something.

Covered as well as I was going to be, I walked back out into the bedroom, stood in the middle of the room, and waited.

I didn't have to wait long.

CHAPTER 5

Serafina

Shadows filled the corners of the room as the moon rose higher in the sky. Every tiny creak or shift of air made me jump as I waited for the beginning of the rest of my life to walk through the door. I kept myself from full out panicking by trying to figure out how many more years my new husband would live and imagining what I would do once I was a widow and free to do as I wanted.

Well, maybe not free. I'd never be completely free from the mafia. Especially not now. But at least I would be able to live alone, and I would be taken care of. As Luigi's only remaining son, Luca would be honor bound to make sure I wanted for nothing once his father was gone. Which meant I would see him often. Luca and his two personal guards.

I immediately pushed the thought of Enzo away. He didn't want me. I wasn't about to let him take up any more space in my head. He could fuck right off as far as I was concerned.

I glanced around the room. The first thing I would do was sell this house and buy something smaller and more to my taste. Then spend whatever was left on furniture and decorations that I liked, because at that moment I realized that I'd never had even a space of my own that was truly me. Even the bedroom I'd grown up in was decorated the same way it had been since I was a child. I'd never thought to ask if I could change it.

When I couldn't stand the silence anymore, I paced the room, my fingers itching with the impulse to pick something up and hide it on my person. Not that I had anywhere to put anything. But my father must've warned him about my little "quirk," because there wasn't so much as a pen lying around. Even in the bathroom, a gaudy explosion of black and gold, there was nothing on the counters except a toothbrush and a tube of toothpaste.

The door opened as I walked out into the bedroom. Luigi stopped in the doorway, his eyes roaming over my body. "You're not my usual type," he told me. "But I suppose you're fuckable enough." His mouth twisted in an expression of dislike. "I'll let you keep that ring in your nose since it's not too gaudy, but that damn pink hair will have to go. I can't be seen with a wife who looks like she just escaped from the circus. I'll have my stylist come do something about it tomorrow."

It was the most he'd said to me since the wedding ceremony.

Shutting the door behind him, he turned the lock, and a chill slithered down my spine. I shivered, trying to pull his shirt closer around me.

Without looking at me again, he walked past me to the closet, pulling off his tie. "I need a son," he announced. "An heir. And you're going to give me one." He hung up his tie on the hanger on the closet wall just inside the door. There was no emotion on his face. Well, maybe annoyance. "Once you've done your duty, I'll give you your own room. But until then, you'll sleep in here."

"But you already have a son," I told him. "You have Luca."

"I do. And he grows more powerful every day. He plans to get rid of me, you know." His dark eyes shifted to me as he laid his cufflinks on the top of the dresser. "But he'll be rethinking that plan now that you're here. Luca is soft when it comes to people he cares about. And he cares about Enzo. He would never do anything to harm you, because he knows his friend would never forgive him if he did."

Nervous as I was, I couldn't help but scoff. "You're wrong. Enzo doesn't give a shit about me."

Luigi's eyebrows rose in amusement. "No? You don't think so?"

"I know so," I told him. "He gave me back to my father."

He unbuttoned his shirt, and my eyes dropped down to his barrel chest covered in gray hairs, only to shoot back up to his face when he said, "And that only proves to me how much he does care. That must be some kind of magic cunt you've got."

This entire day had me mentally exhausted, and I frowned in confusion. I wasn't very experienced in the dating scene, but it seemed pretty common sense to me that if a guy cared about you, he wouldn't throw you away.

"Take off my shirt. You look ridiculous. Then get on the bed." He paused, tilting his head as he looked me over one more time. "Leave the nightgown on." Turning his back, he walked into the bathroom in nothing but his slacks and shoes, calling over his shoulder, "And if you touch my cufflinks, I'll cut off your hands. They were a gift." The door closed behind him, and I heard the shower come on.

So he *was* aware of my little habit. My eyes shot to the bedroom door, then the window, then back to the door as adrenaline rushed through my bloodstream. But I knew that even if I managed to make it out of the house, I wouldn't get off the property. He probably had guards stationed out in the hall and in the yard below the bedroom. Tears filled my eyes, and I blinked them away. *Come on, Sera. It's time to toughen up. You've been through worse than this and survived. You'll survive this, too.*

But what if I couldn't give him a son? What would he do to me? My birth control pills were in my bags that should've been here by now, so they must be in the house somewhere. If they weren't discovered, I could continue to take them, and maybe he'd get tired of trying to get me pregnant and leave me alone. Or maybe he'd kill me and bury me in his flowerbed.

No. He'd just admitted that one of the reasons I was here was because he thought I'd serve as some kind of protection against Luca. And even though I knew it not to be true, if it would keep me alive, I wasn't going to argue with him about it.

The water cut off, and I knew my time was running out. But I'd be damned if I was going to be draped across the bed waiting for him in this ridiculous excuse for sleepwear. So I stayed exactly where I was.

He wore nothing but a towel wrapped around his waist when he came out, his bow legs sticking out from the bottom, the nails on his toes thick and yellowed with age. I schooled my features so he wouldn't see the disgust I felt.

"I see I'm going to have to teach you how to obey commands." He didn't sound put out about it. Quite the opposite, actually. Walking over to his dresser, he opened a small drawer on the top I didn't notice before and pulled out a thick leather belt.

My heart jumped into my throat.

"Take off the shirt and get on the fucking bed."

My immediate reaction was to tell him to fuck off, and I hesitated for just a moment. But that was all it took. Between one second and the next, he'd crossed the eight feet or so between us and I heard the belt whistle through the air right before it landed across my arm and shoulder with a sharp, burning sting that made me cry out.

Fury rose inside of me.

"Take off the shirt," he ordered again.

"No," I sneered. Defying him was stupid of me and wasn't going to bring me anything but more pain and misery, but I couldn't seem to stop myself.

The belt whipped through the air again, only this time I was prepared and twisted my body away from it. I wasn't quite fast enough though, and it landed on my hip and wrapped around my ass, leaving a burning strip of skin through the thin material of the nightgown that hurt way worse than the first hit.

"Take. Off. The. Shirt!" he shouted.

"No!" I shouted back, bracing myself for another hit. I was backed up against the end of the bed, my eyes darting to either side, searching for an escape route. But I knew I wouldn't get far even if I did manage to get around him. My blood boiled in my veins, and I wondered how much of a chance I'd have of wrestling the belt away from him. He was a man far from his prime, but he still had a lot of strength, as my stinging skin could attest to.

"I'll whip the skin from your bones, girl. Don't think I won't!"

"Sera," I gritted out between my teeth.

He frowned. "What?"

"My *name* is Sera."

"I know what your fucking name is, girl. Now take off that shirt and get on the bed before I call in my men to hold you down. I'm growing tired of your games."

If I was smart, I would do as he told me and stop fighting with him. I was only making things harder on myself by not doing what he demanded, and in the end, I wouldn't win. I knew this. And yet, for some reason, I couldn't bring myself to stop. Maybe it was a delayed reaction to all the things I was put through in Mexico. Maybe I was just sick and fucking tired of men trying to tell me what to fucking do. Of using me. Only to throw me out like trash when they were done with me.

Opening my mouth, I screamed and lunged for him, one hand going for the belt. But he avoided my hand and then backhanded me across the face. His ring slammed into my cheekbone, and I bit down on my cheek right before I went flying, landing on my knees on the hard floor. Pain jarred up my legs and across my face, and I tasted the coppery tang of blood.

"You fucking bitch!" Luigi stood over me, and I glanced up just in time to see him swing the belt toward my face. I ducked and covered my head, and it glanced off the back of my hands. But he recovered quickly, and I felt the crack of leather across my back.

I braced myself for another blow, but it never happened. The sound of shattered glass came from behind me, and I peeked up to find Luigi frozen in place with the belt above his head. He dropped his arm and started to laugh.

"Do not touch her again."

The voice was so cold I felt slivers of ice slide over my burning skin, but it was also very familiar. So very familiar. Yet I had nothing to say to him, so I stayed where I was on the floor, although I did sit up onto my knees, wincing when they protested the change in weight, and wiped the tears from my face and the blood from my mouth.

There was a knock on the bedroom door. "Boss?"

"I'm fine," Luigi answered. "Stay where you are." He didn't move away from me. "I was wondering when you were going to show up. Honestly, Enzo, I was disappointed when you didn't try to stop the wedding."

He sighed dramatically. "But instead, you decided to interrupt my wedding night."

I heard the buzz of a cell phone vibrating, and then it stopped. A second later, it buzzed again.

"I can only assume from the fact that someone is frantically calling you that my son doesn't know you are here."

"No."

Still standing over me, Luigi threw his arms wide, the belt dangling near my face. I cringed away. "So? Now what, boy? What are you going to do?"

The silence in the room was palpable. I glanced over my shoulder. Enzo's hands were fisted at his sides, his teeth clenched together so tightly I could hear the enamel grinding off. But other than that...

Nothing. He was going to do nothing.

Luigi cocked his head. "All these dramatics...breaking my window...and for what, Enzo? For nothing."

"Not for nothing. Sera is *mine*."

My heart skipped a beat, my body traitorous, as always. But it didn't matter. I was Luigi's wife now. It was too late. *He* was too late.

"Yours?" Luigi laughed again, and then sobered just as quickly. "If I ordered you to kill her right now, you would. Just like you killed Alessandra."

"No."

"Don't fuck with me, boy. Your loyalty is to your family. It always has been, and it always will be." His voice lowered. "It's why I trusted you with my son. You would die for him. I know that, and so does he."

"So would Tristan."

But Luigi shook his head. "Tristan would throw himself in front of a bullet because he doesn't care if he lives or dies, this is true. But if he found someone who could take his pain away, he would betray Luca's trust in a heartbeat. Unlike you, Enzo, he would choose. And something as trivial as loyalty to the family wouldn't weigh on his conscience." He walked around until he was standing in front of me, my face at the same level as his groin. He did it on purpose to make his point. I scooted back out of his reach, not that it would stop him from ordering me to suck him off in front of Enzo if he'd get a kick out of it.

"You don't know Tristan," Enzo told him. "And you don't know me."

"I think I do, boy. Now get the fuck out of my room and let me finish consummating my marriage." Looking down at me for the first time since Enzo broke into the room, Luigi took a step toward me and grabbed me by the hair. I cried out as he started to lift me to my feet.

"I *told* you not to touch her again." The warning came right before his gun went off behind me.

I jumped and screamed, my eyes going to Luigi's face. There was a bullet hole in the center of his forehead. A second later, his grip on my hair loosened and he fell to the floor in front of me, his cell phone falling out of his pocket and sliding across the floor. Impulsively, I grabbed it.

The bedroom door handle rattled. "Boss! Boss! What's going on in there?"

"We need to go," Enzo told me quietly. A jacket was thrown over my shoulders and I was hauled to my feet. "We need to go *now*."

My feet tried to gain purchase on the floor as he dragged me back toward the broken window. "Let me go!" My mind spun with everything that had just happened. "Let me go!"

Ignoring my protests, he grabbed me around the waist and forced me over to the window. Lifting me easily, he sent me out feet first onto the roof, never letting go of me as he followed me out.

"Enzo! Stop!"

His hand slammed down over my mouth, and he held me in front of him as he took me over to the corner of the roofline where a tree grew over the house. "Hang on," he told me, using his strength and body weight to force me out onto a thick branch. I noticed for the first time that he was barefoot, and the hand that covered my mouth was slippery with blood. I didn't know if it was his or mine.

Once we were out on the branch, he scanned the yard below us. "You can hang onto me and keep your mouth shut," he said quietly in my ear, "or I'll throw you off this branch. Either way, you're coming with me to the ground. If you scream and bring Luigi's men over here, all you're going to do is get us both killed."

Grudgingly, I nodded. He wasn't leaving me much choice. Luigi's guards would shoot first and ask questions later. And I didn't want to die.

Enzo took his hand away from my mouth and turned me around, one hand hanging onto the branch above us. "Put your arms and legs around me and hang on."

I did as he said, wincing as my body screamed in protest where Luigi had beaten me. Enzo began to scale his way down the tree. Above us, I heard the bedroom door bust open.

Enzo froze, and his eyes met mine. A look of determination crossed his features. "Don't let go," he said quietly.

And then he jumped.

CHAPTER 6

Enzo

Sera's submissive behavior only lasted as long as it took me to get her off of Luigi's property. As soon as we were far enough down the street near where I'd parked the car I'd rented under a fake name, she yanked her hand from mine, turned, and ran down a side street.

I cursed under my breath and took off after her, catching up to her easily and lifting her into my arms. "Where the hell do you think you're going?" I kept my voice down, and so did she as she struggled in my grip.

"Let me go, you son of a bitch!"

Turning her in my arms, I threw her over my shoulder and stalked back to the car, keeping a watchful eye for any nosy neighbors. Luckily, it was late enough that most people were settled in for the night. Which was good for them, because if any man wandered out of his house and saw Sera running down the street practically naked, I'd have to kill him just for looking at her.

She pummeled me with her fists everywhere she could reach. When I got tired of it, I slapped her hard on the ass. She froze in shock, but only for a moment before she started in again. "Jesus fucking Christ." I started to jog down the street, and she was forced to hang on or bounce off my shoulder. I smiled when I felt her clutch the back of my shirt.

When we reached the corner, I stopped and checked the surrounding area. All seemed quiet, but just in case, I pulled my gun from its holster and clicked off the safety. Adjusting Sera on my shoulder, I hurried across the street to the car, my eyes scanning the area for any sign of Luigi's men.

I'd left the doors on the rental unlocked. Opening the driver's side, I dumped Sera into the car and climbed in after her. I kept a tight hold on her wrist, just in case she got it into her pretty head to jump out the other side, and reached over the steering wheel to shift it into neutral. Leaving the headlights off, I took my foot off the brake. The car started to roll down the hill.

Sera used her other hand to try to pry mine off of her wrist. "Let go of me! Let me out of this fucking car!" Now that we were out of hearing range, she had no qualms about letting me know exactly how she felt.

"Stop it," I ordered. We didn't have time for this shit. She could be mad at me once I had us both somewhere safe. We reached the bottom of the hill and I let go of her to start the engine. But first, I locked the doors. And just in time. As soon as I released her, Sera lunged for the door handle just as I threw the car into drive. She was fast, but I was faster. Before she could get the door open, I grabbed her by the back of the neck and hauled her back over to me. Holding her tight against my chest, I pressed a kiss to her forehead as she tried to shove me away. I couldn't fucking believe she was here beside me again.

My hands were shaking, Sera's curses and protests fading into the background as the full realization of what I'd just done crashed over me.

I'd just killed Luca's father.

I'd just killed the boss.

This wasn't my plan when I'd driven over here. Originally, I'd just wanted to make sure she was okay. I'd left my dress shoes in the car and climbed onto the roof outside of Luigi's room. I'd wanted to reassure myself that she was okay. Luigi wasn't a gentle man, and he had little respect for women.

That's what I told myself. But in truth, I was a masochist. I'd known when I'd turned her back over to her father that she would be sold to the highest bidder. I'd fucking known it. And I'd done it anyway. Because I was a son of a bitch who was too fucking afraid to love her. Because I wanted her to be safe. And I knew she wouldn't be safe with me, not as long as she wanted out of this life.

Luigi would never let me out. And as soon as he saw that Sera was a distraction to me, he would take the one I loved from me again. So, I'd given her up to keep her away from him, and the whole thing had blown up in my fucking face.

I was scared of what I would see when I climbed onto that roof.

Instead, I saw my girl rise up like some kind of pissed off goddess and go after him, and I was so proud. And relieved. Until he raised his belt and beat her down.

That was all it took. Before I could think about what I was doing, my fist went through the window, making a hole, and then another, until the opening was big enough that my body took out the rest when I dove into the room and rolled to my feet. After that, there was no way in fucking hell I was leaving her there with him.

"Are you okay?" I asked her. I glanced down. Her curvy legs were completely visible through the non-existent gown he had her in, and my cock grew stiff. "Sera?"

She'd finally tired of trying to get away from me and was now sitting tucked into my side with her arms crossed over her chest, her face turned away, holding my jacket close around her. "I'm cold," she muttered.

"Turn on the heater. Right there." I lifted my chin toward the console. I would do it myself, but I didn't trust her not to jump from the vehicle as soon as I let go of her. And being that we were now on the highway, I couldn't allow that to happen.

"Where are we going?" she asked as she cranked on the heater.

"I don't know."

Right on cue, my cell vibrated in my pocket. I ignored it.

"You can let me go."

"So you can jump out of the car?" I laughed, but the sound held no humor. "No."

"I'm not fucking suicidal, Enzo. And my back hurts sitting like this."

Immediately, I released her neck, remembering how hard Luigi had hit her. "I'm sorry. I didn't mean to hurt you."

My phone vibrated again. Just once this time. With a side glance at Sera to make sure she wasn't going to try anything, I pulled it from my pocket and checked the screen. It was from Luca.

Answer your goddamn phone.

IMMEDIATELY AFTER, his number flashed across my screen. I stared at it for a long moment, my mind racing. I didn't want to implicate him any more than I had to with this. But I also knew he wouldn't give up until he talked to me. I tapped the screen and answered the call.

"What the hell did you do, Enzo?" he growled before I could say anything. I wasn't surprised that he already knew what had happened. Luca had his spies everywhere, even in his father's own home.

I glanced at Sera again. She was staring out the passenger side window with her arms crossed over her chest, her legs and feet practically bare, with only the thin gown covering them. Her silence was making me nervous. "He was hurting her. I couldn't leave her there with him," I confessed, still watching her. Although she didn't move, I saw her stiffen slightly. "I couldn't leave her," I repeated. "I couldn't let him have her."

Luca sighed heavily. "Did anyone see either of you?"

"No."

"You're absolutely sure?"

"Yes. Although I may have left some blood in the bedroom. My blood."

He was quiet for a long moment. "You know they're going to think she did this."

I did. That's why I was running with her. "I know."

"Where are you now?"

"Driving." I didn't need to tell him anything more. Luca knew me better than anyone.

"You need to come back here. Bring Sera. We can hide her. My father's men won't find her here."

"I can't do that, Luca. It's too dangerous."

"You must. It'll look too suspicious otherwise. There'll be a meeting of the family to vote on the new boss as soon as possible. You have to be there. We'll come up with a scenario that will remove all blame from her."

"No. It's too risky. She's a witness, Luca. I'm taking her out of here. She can't be anywhere near this city."

"So you're just going to run for the rest of your life. Is that the plan? Because if it is, it's a stupid plan."

"It's the only choice I have right now."

"No, Enzo. It's not," he said softly. "You have us. We'll help you protect your Sera."

My Sera. "Luca—"

"Bring her home, Enz. I swear to you on my life, I won't let anything happen to her."

"Your father is dead," I blurted. Whether to drive that fact home to him or to myself, I couldn't say.

"I know. Bring her home, Enzo."

I ended the call and looked around me. I didn't even know where the fuck I was. I'd been driving blindly, my only thought being to get her the hell away from that house.

"Are we going back to Luca's?" she asked me quietly.

She was still angry with me. I could hear it in her voice. What if I got her somewhere and she tried to run from me? She would attract attention, and then I would have to kill more people, leaving a trail of bodies for Luigi's loyal followers to track us.

I thought about what Luca had said, trying to push my panic aside and think logically. No one knew where Luca's house was, not even his father. Luca had made it that way as soon as his power began to rival his father's. If I took her there, it would give us time we didn't have right now. Time to figure out how to remove their suspicion from Sera.

"Enzo?"

"Yes," I told her. I pulled off the next exit and went west toward the lakes.

She straightened in her seat. "I don't want to go back there."

"We have to."

"No. We don't."

"We can't run forever."

"I wouldn't have to run at all if it wasn't for you."

"Would you rather I'd left you there to be beaten into submission like a fucking dog?" I asked her.

She threw up her hands. "Yes!" When I gave her a skeptical look, she added, "I could've handled Luigi."

I shook my head. "You're delusional if you believe that." He would've beaten her down until that spirit that lit her up from the inside was extinguished forever.

Sarcasm dripped from her voice when she said, "Believe it or not, I actually have some experience dealing with psychotic old men."

"At least your father didn't fuck you."

"Who I fuck or don't fuck isn't any of your business anymore."

My hand shot out and grabbed her wrist. I yanked her toward me as far as the seatbelt would allow until her face was only inches from mine. "That's where you're wrong, baby girl. *I* am the only man who will fuck you."

"You didn't want me," she spit out. Her blue-gray eyes shiny with tears.

"I just killed a man to save you!"

"I don't need you to save me," she sneered. "I can save myself." She yanked her wrist out of my grip, and I let her go.

"Sera..."

But she shook her head. "Don't, Enzo."

I sighed deeply. I'd deal with her attitude later. Right now, I needed to concentrate on getting her somewhere safe.

We made the rest of the trip in silence. When we arrived at Luca's, I pulled off the side of the road and texted him, waiting until he gave me the all clear before going up to the house.

He was waiting for us when we arrived back at the lake house. When we walked into the house, he was there in the middle of the great room, standing all alone, his hands fisted at his sides. But when he spoke, his tone was even. "Where is the car you used?"

"In the garage."

His blue eyes took a quick assessment of us both. Sera, in the black see-through gown, a dress shirt, and my jacket, her mouth smeared with blood from my hand. And me, with blood covering my hands and shirt from the broken glass. "Whose phone is that?" he asked her.

Phone? What phone?

Sera held it out to him. "Your father's. I'm sorry. I tend to steal things when I'm upset. It's like a nervous tic I can't get rid of."

Luca took it from her, turning it this way and that. He tucked it into his inside jacket pocket. "Thank you, Sera. Would you please excuse us? I believe if you go upstairs, Veda is waiting for you in our bedroom. She'll help you get cleaned up and into some decent clothes if you wish." He nodded toward my hand, once again clasped around her wrist. "Let her go, Enzo."

I took a steadying breath and did as he ordered. Then I watched as she climbed the stairs in her bare feet, only looking back at me once before she disappeared down the hall toward Luca and Veda's room.

"Is she a flight risk?"

My eyes flicked back to my friend. "Yes."

He nodded, unsurprised. "I'll let the guards know no one is to leave this house without my permission. We'll need to be cautious until the question of my father's death and his replacement is settled." He turned his father's cell phone around in his hands and tapped the screen, trying a few passwords. "As soon as Tristan gets back, we'll have him break into this phone and see what we can find." His eyes rose to mine, and he smiled, but it was strained. "Maybe we'll get lucky."

"I'm sorry," I told him sincerely.

He met my gaze, and his eyes searched mine for a long time.

"I tried to stay away," I said. "I did. I just wanted to make sure she was okay."

A strange look crossed his features. "I assume my father was wooing her into his bed with his usual manner of brutality."

"He was beating her with a thick leather belt."

Luca was silent for a moment, but I saw the rage in his eyes. A rage that came nowhere near to matching mine. "I can't blame you for what you did, Enzo. If it had been Veda, I would've done the same. What happened has happened. There's no going back now. All we can do is try to control the fallout."

"It was your *father*," I insisted, as if that meant something. And it should. I'd lost both of my parents when I was very young, but I would think it should mean something.

"My father was a monster who didn't give a shit about me. Why should I give a shit about him?" But he did care. I could see it in his eyes and the tightness around his mouth. "In any case, we don't have time for this right now. You can beg my forgiveness later. Go get yourself cleaned up, then take those clothes outside and burn them."

"Luca—"

But he cut me off. "You're covered in blood, Enz. Go." Taking the phone with him, he headed to his office, his shoulders slumped with grief he wouldn't acknowledge.

Turning on my heel, I went to do as he'd ordered. As I climbed the stairs, I lifted my hands out in front of me.

They were shaking again.

CHAPTER 7

Serafina

I knew he would come and find me, so even though I desperately wanted to take a shower and change into the clothes Veda had given me, I sat on the bed and waited after washing the smears of blood from around my mouth.

The ring that was still on my finger sparkled in the light. I'd become a wife and a widow on the same day. My husband—I choked down the hysterical laughter that rose in my throat—killed in cold blood right in front of me. And I felt...nothing.

No anger. No regret. No relief. No joy.

Nothing.

Time slowed as I heard Enzo's footsteps approaching the room we'd shared before he so carelessly discarded me. They stopped right outside the door.

My heart too loud in my ears, I watched the doorknob. It seemed to take forever, but finally, I heard the slight rattle of metal, the knob turned, and the door opened.

Enzo strode into the room as though he hadn't had that moment's hesitation before he came in. What was he afraid of, I wondered? His eyes found me immediately, sitting there on the edge of the bed, waiting for him. He was still wearing the bloody clothes he'd shown up in.

He stopped just inside the door, reaching behind him to close it. "How are you feeling?"

Nothing. I felt nothing.

When I didn't answer him, he chewed on the inside of his cheek, studying me. His eyes, completely visible without his sunglasses, roamed over my face before they dropped down to the rest of my body. Though my skin burned everywhere they touched, I held perfectly still. There was no way in hell I was going to allow him to see how much he affected me. Not if I could help it.

"Did he hurt you badly?"

"Yes," I told him. There was no reason to lie about it. My body still ached everywhere Luigi's belt had struck me. I'd probably be black and blue in the morning if I wasn't already.

The muscles in Enzo's jaw flexed. "I wish I could kill him again. Only this time I wouldn't let my temper get the best of me and I'd break him apart, piece by piece."

"Why did you come there?" I asked him, despite the promise I'd made to myself to hate him. But I wanted to know. I *needed* to know. Was this some stupid macho man bullshit? Or was it something more?

"Because you're *mine*, Sera."

I did laugh then. It was an ugly sound. "Yours?" I repeated incredulously when I could speak.

His eyes narrowed in on me. "Yes."

I was so fucking confused. "Do you always give away your property and then kill the man you gave it to and take it back?" A thought occurred to me. "Is it the hunt? Is that it? Does the chase excite you? And then once it's over, you lose interest?"

He was shaking his head before I finished speaking. "No, baby. That's not it at all."

I would've stood up then so he could feel the full force of my disgust with him, but my back ached from the beating Luigi gave me. "Then explain it to me," I told him. "Explain to me why a man who was willing to pay an ungodly amount of money just to talk me into spending time with him and who would go all the way to *fucking* Mexico to save me suddenly wants nothing to do with me."

"It was safer for you to go back to your father than to stay here with me."

"Why?"

He stared at me, his dark eyes burning with so many emotions they seared me through to the bone and made me catch my breath.

"Tell me why, Enzo."

"Because I didn't want to have to choose."

"Choose what?"

"Between you and my family."

I stared at him. I thought I knew where he was going with this, but I needed to hear him say it. "Why would you have to?"

"Because you're a distraction to me, and Luigi wouldn't like that. Because you want to get away from this life. Just like Alessandra."

It all clicked into place. The rumors I'd heard about him were true. The whispers. Everyone was afraid of him because he felt nothing. So cold-hearted he murdered his own wife. "And you killed her," I said softly.

Surprise flashed across his face that I knew, but only for a moment. "I did," he admitted.

Chills chased each other up and down my spine. "Why?" I'd always wanted to know what would drive a man to kill the woman he loved, the mother of his child.

"Because Luigi ordered me to do it."

"And you always follow orders," I surmised, "no matter what that order might be."

"Alessandra had become a liability," he continued. "A danger to the family. She blamed him for the death of our son, and she wanted revenge. Other than locking her in a room, which I didn't want to do, I couldn't control her. I kept hoping that she would snap out of it, but she only got worse. Eventually, she would've endangered me or someone else. So he ordered the hit."

"Why did he ask you to do it?"

His expression remained completely impassive, as did his voice. But there was an unforgotten fury in his eyes. "It was a chance for me to prove to him that my loyalty still lied with him and the family."

I frowned. "What about *your* family? She was your *wife*, Enzo."

"You think I don't know that?" he asked me. "You think I didn't want to put a gun to my head and join them?"

"So why didn't you?"

He recoiled from my question. Not physically. But I could feel it. It was a cruel thing to ask, but right now I didn't feel like I owed him any sympathy.

I thought I saw something flash across his face before his dark eyes went almost black. His chest rose and fell with every labored breath, straining the buttons on the shirt he wore. "Because Luca made me swear I wouldn't."

"And you do whatever Luca tells you to do." I couldn't keep the sarcasm from my voice.

His eyes hardened. "Luca is my boss. And more than that, he's my friend." He cocked his head to the side. "Is that what you wish, Sera? That you'd never met me? That I'd stuck the barrel of my gun in my mouth and blown my fucking head off?"

No, of course not. I'd never wish that for anybody.

And especially not for him. The sharp ache in my chest just thinking of it was so painful it made it impossible for me to breathe.

He stepped closer to me, so close he towered over me where I sat on the bed. One hand cradled the side of my face and lifted it up until I was forced to look at him. "Is that what you want, baby girl?"

Silently, I shook my head.

"I never should've done what I did," he said quietly. "Jesus, Sera..." His eyes burned into me as they traveled over my face, settling on my lips, and when he spoke again, his voice was little more than a whisper. "You terrify me more than anyone else in my life. I'm *terrified*, Sera. Even now."

I didn't understand. Why would he be afraid of me?

But it didn't matter. Not anymore. None of this mattered anymore. He'd turned his back on me. Given me back to the very monster I'd tried so hard to escape from as though it was nothing. As though *I* was nothing. And I wasn't about to forgive him just because he had a fear of commitment.

I wasn't afraid of him, though, and that was kind of fucked up. He'd just admitted to me that he'd killed his wife in cold blood because he'd been ordered to. And yet, the only thing I really wanted to do right now was to lean forward into his hard strength and let him take care of me.

It was insane. I knew that. How I trusted him with my body. But I couldn't trust him with my heart.

Pulling my face away from his hand, I broke eye contact. "I'm exhausted, and I'd like to get cleaned up and go to bed now. I don't want to talk anymore."

"I can help you."

"No." I shook my head. "I don't want you in here."

"At least let me make sure none of your injuries are serious."

"They're not," I told him. "I've had much worse." From my father, for one. "I just want you to go."

I felt his stare, heavy and hot, and I fully expected him to argue with me or just do whatever he wanted to do with me anyway. But to my surprise, after a long pause, he stepped back. "I'll be in the next room. If you change your mind, or you need anything at all, just call out."

"I won't," I told him, lifting my eyes back to his face.

After a moment, he went into the closet and returned with a few items of clothes. "I'll be in the next room," he repeated. Then he turned on his heel and left, closing the door behind him.

As soon as the door was closed, I rose painfully to my feet and hobbled into the bathroom. Sitting for so long had left me feeling stiff. Bending over to turn on the bath water made my breath catch and tears fill my eyes, but I managed. Carefully, I removed Enzo's jacket and Luigi's shirt, wishing I could burn them both.

I was glad Luigi was dead. Tomorrow I would worry about the consequences of what Enzo had done, but for right now, I just wanted to soak in the bath and then go to bed.

Gathering the barely-there material of the nightgown in my hands, I tried to lift it up over my head. Burning pain shot across my right shoulder blade where the belt had torn into my skin. I gasped, dropping my arms again, and changed tactics. But the material wasn't stretchy enough to slide it off my shoulders easily.

I started opening and closing drawers, looking for a knife, a razor blade, anything I could use to cut the damn thing off of me. When I couldn't find anything, I tried to rip it, but I wasn't strong enough.

Tears streamed down my face. I had to get this damn thing off. I couldn't stand the feel of it on my skin anymore. I moved to the other side of the sink and started yanking open more drawers, pulling so hard one came completely out and fell onto the floor with a crash. My head jerked up, and I caught my reflection in the large mirror over the sink—a crazy woman with makeup running down her face in streaks, exposing a black eye, and red welts forming on her shoulders.

In a fucking black, see-through nightgown. A nightgown I was beaten in, and no doubt would've been raped in.

Opening my mouth, I screamed at the woman in the mirror, my hands tugging at the gown and then at my hair when I couldn't get it off.

The bathroom door flew open so fast it slammed into the wall behind it and Enzo was there, forcing my hands out of my hair and taking me into his strong arms. I couldn't move, which meant I couldn't get out of this damned nightgown. "Get it off!" I yelled, crazy now. "Get it the fuck off of me!"

Enzo didn't hesitate. His strong hands gripped the neckline at my back and tugged. I sobbed with relief when the material gave. He tore it from me like it was soaked in acid, and I heard his soft curse as it fell to the floor at my feet. Looking up, I saw his eyes on the mirror behind me. He was staring at my back, and judging by the pain I felt, I could imagine what he saw. Though he practically vibrated with rage, his voice was low and controlled when he told me, "I'm not leaving. So tell me what you're trying to do."

I was too exhausted, both mentally and physically, to argue with him. "Take a bath and go to sleep. *Alone*," I added. Pushing him away from me, I crossed my arms over my naked breasts. I wouldn't look at him. If I did, he would see the conflict in my eyes. Because a part of me— the part that was hurt and fed up and done with his shit— couldn't stand the feel of his hands. But the other part of me just wanted to fall into his arms and allow him to take care of me. To love me. Even if it was only a pretense.

I felt his eyes burning into my bare skin on my shoulders, my stomach, and lower. "Okay." His voice was deep and husky. "We can do that. And I'm helping you."

"I don't need your help now that that stupid thing is off."

"Well, that's too fucking bad, Sera, because you're getting it."

CHAPTER 8

Enzo

The soft, tender skin of Sera's back was red, and welts had risen where Luigi's belt had struck her, mostly on her right side, from her shoulder blade down to her hip. And since I'd already killed the man responsible, all I could do was stand there and vibrate with rage that anyone would do this to her. He had no fucking right. Sera was not his. And the only thing that made me feel the slightest bit better was knowing that now she never would be.

With effort, I tore my eyes away from her abused skin. The water in the tub was getting too high, so I walked over and shut it off. Then I found some Epsom salts under the sink and poured some into the hot water. There were no open wounds on her that I saw, just bruised skin with raised welts, so it should be okay. When I was done, I held out my hand. "Come on."

She eyed it like I was holding a snake poised to strike, and as the light struck her face just right, I thought I saw purplish bruising around her eye. After a moment, she took my hand and allowed me to help her into the bath. Carefully, she lowered herself into the tub, letting out a hiss when the water touched her back.

"Is it too hot?"

"No." She shook her head and eased herself further down into the tub until she was fully submerged. "Is Luca angry with me for stealing his father's phone?"

"No," I told her. "Not at all. We're hoping there will be something on it that will help us justify his murder and clear your name."

My cock swelled watching the water dance over her bare breasts, but I ignored it. I wasn't a total monster. Walking over to the medicine cabinet, I grabbed her a couple of Advil and the bottled water Lisa always left on the bathroom counter.

She glanced at me sideways when I held them out to her. "Stop looking at me like that."

I squatted down beside the tub until we were nearly face to face. She most definitely had a black eye. From Luigi, I would assume. And there was a small cut on her cheekbone. "Like what?"

"Like you feel sorry for me. I've had worse." She took the pills and water from me and swallowed them down. "Thank you."

My blood began to boil at her casual admission. "I didn't see marks on you like this when I took you from Mexico."

A haunted look passed over her perfect face, there and gone within a few beats of my heart as she handed the water back to me. "I'm not talking about that."

"Then what?"

"Why the hell do you think I wanted to get away from my father so badly?

Slowly, I rose to my feet and set the bottle back on the counter in case she needed it. Through clenched teeth, I asked her, "What exactly has your father done to you, Sera?"

She stared at the wall in front of her. "He's done a lot of things. None of which I want to go into detail about."

"He hurt you when I sent you back." It wasn't a question. I knew now who had given her the shiner.

She looked at me then, her light eyes darkened with memories. "Yes," she said simply. "And then he sold me off to Luigi, for a discounted price, I'm sure, since I'm now damaged goods. Which was my own choice," she was quick to add. "At least the first time. I don't blame you for that."

I stared down at this woman that I was foolish enough to think I could live without. "You're not damaged."

She didn't respond, but I could tell by the look on her face she was less than convinced. She sighed heavily. "So what happens now?"

The urge to commit a second murder that night was still strong within me, but I couldn't leave her. Not right now. "You're going to need to stay here again for a while."

"Until you can ship me back to my father again?"

"I'm not going to do that."

"What are you going to do then? Find me a new husband yourself?"

"No, Sera."

She looked up at me. "So I'm a prisoner here until when?"

"You're not a prisoner. But you need to stay here so we can keep you safe. Luigi's men think you killed him and escaped out the window. And we need to keep it that way. Just for now. Until we can be sure there won't be any retaliation for his death."

She looked back at the wall. "I would have. Eventually. He was a bastard."

I smiled a little for the first time in a long time. My bloodthirsty little warrior. There was no doubt in my mind she was telling the truth.

In the next second, she wiped the smile right off my face. "I need you to leave now. I don't want to talk to you anymore."

"That's just too fucking bad, baby, because I'm staying right here." I cocked my head, contemplating her profile as a thought occurred to me. "Are you planning to kill me, too?"

She looked away.

"I'm a bastard, too. I'm the son of a bitch who made you promises I didn't keep. Who sent you back to your abusive father so he could sell you off to an abusive husband." I squatted next to her again so I could brush her cheek with the backs of my fingers. Just a soft touch. But it was enough to get a reaction from both of us. The light glinted off her silver nose ring as her nostrils flared slightly on a sharp inhale of breath. "What are you going to do to *me*, baby girl?"

She turned her head, and her eyes clashed with mine. Damp tendrils of pink hair curled around her face, sticking to her temples. Her cheeks, neck, and chest were flushed red from the heat of the bath water, and her eyes were bright and still slightly glazed over with pain.

"Are you going to kill me, too?" I asked her again.

I watched as tears filled her eyes.

"I would understand if you did," I told her, and I meant it. My only regret would be that I would no longer get to touch her soft skin, or hear the music of her laugh, something I haven't heard in quite a long time. I'd never again get to watch as her back arched with pleasure. Never hear the sounds she made when she was close to orgasm. Those things, I would miss too much.

Hell, I'd even miss the way she wasn't afraid to stand up to me. Very few men had the balls to do that, and yet this little girl had pulled my own gun on me. And she probably would've shot me, too, if I hadn't gotten it away from her.

I turned my hand so that my palm was cupping the side of her head, and watched as a tear slid silently down her cheek. I brushed it away with my thumb. "I've missed you," I confessed.

Her expression hardened, and I took her mouth with mine before she could tell me to leave again. She pressed her lips together, refusing to let me in, even as a whimper of need escaped her throat. My other hand wrapped around her throat. I tilted her head up, using my tongue to push my way between her lips until she finally opened for me. And then I was inside, thrusting my tongue into her mouth. I moaned when I tasted her. The only thing that tasted better than Sera's mouth was her pussy.

I tasted the salt of her tears as I kissed her, but she didn't try to push me away. I moved my hand from her throat and dipped it beneath the water, finding her breasts. Her nipples were hard, straining for my palm when I brushed it over them, and a surge of blood rushed to my cock. I went lower, over her soft belly to the wet curls of hair that covered her pussy. I cupped her in my palm as I slid my middle finger between her soft folds to find her clit.

Pulling my mouth from hers just enough so I could talk, I whispered against her lips, "I want to make you come. But you gotta let me know if I'm hurting you. Comprendere?" *Understand?*

"Yes," she whispered back. Her eyes were on mine, the pupils so large they appeared almost black.

"Hang onto the side of the tub."

Obediently, she raised her arms out of the water as I leaned forward on my knees and tightened my grip on her damp hair. With my other hand, I squeezed her pussy, then started to work her clit with two fingers. She was wet, both with the water in the tub and the slickness of her own arousal.

She could hate me all she wanted, but she couldn't deny that she wanted my touch.

I turned my face so I could look down the length of her lush body, the image wavy but clear beneath the water. "You're so fucking beautiful, Sera." And I meant it. I'd never seen a woman more perfectly made for me than she was. I slid a finger deep inside of her, curling it around to rub the sensitive part of her inner wall. "I want to feel you come on my fingers. I want to watch your face when you fall apart."

She cried out softly at my words.

I wanted to lift her from the water and bring her sweet breasts to my mouth, but I was afraid I'd hurt her back. So I kept her floating, holding her head off the hard side of the tub and allowing the water to support her body. The zipper of my pants was digging hard into my cock, but that was okay. Maybe it would keep me from soaking the inside of my pants with my come.

Her hands tightened on the side of the tub and her breaths were coming fast and hard. I went back to her clit, her back arching when I touched her just right. My eyes went back to her face. "Easy," I told her when she winced. "I've got you, baby girl."

The red flush on her chest deepened, and I knew she was close. My balls tightened just watching her. "Come for me, Sera," I ordered. A rush of pleasure zipped down my spine as she did as I commanded, her lips brushing mine as her hips rose from the water right before her body jerked in on itself and she cried out against my mouth.

"Yes, baby. That's it. Ah! God, Sera..." My cock swelled tight as my orgasm rushed up its length and spilled out into my boxer briefs. "Fuck." The curse came out on a moan as I humped the side of the tub, wishing like hell it was her tight pussy milking me dry.

I pressed my forehead to hers as we breathed each other's air, chests heaving. "Do you want me to kill him?"

It took her a few seconds to ask, "Who?"

"Your father."

Sera's eyes blinked open, and she pulled away so she could look at me.

"I'll go find him right now, and he'll no longer be a problem for you ever again," I promised.

I saw the conflict in her eyes, and for a moment I thought she was going to say yes. But then she shook her head. "No."

I inhaled and exhaled through my nose, trying to calm the beast inside of me who was screaming for vengeance for her. "If you change your mind, all you have to do is say the word."

She stared at me for a minute, but I couldn't read her expression. "I want to wash and get out now."

Untangling my fingers from her hair and giving the soft flesh between her legs one last feel, I rose to my feet. I saw her eyes drop to the wet stain on the front of my slacks before she quickly averted them to grab the soap. In the closet, I stripped out of my bloody clothes, using my boxer briefs to clean myself up, then pulled on a pair of gray sweats. I grabbed one of my T-shirts from the drawer for Sera. I'd take a shower later.

When I returned to the bathroom, she was standing in the tub with a towel wrapped around her and was attempting to get out of the tub. "Hey, hey. Let me help you." Dropping the shirt on the floor, I reached for her, stopping cold when she slapped my hand away.

"I don't need your help, Enzo. I don't want your help." She looked at me with disgust in her swollen eyes. She'd washed her makeup off, and her black eye was plain to see now. "I can't help the way my body reacts to you, but I'll be damned if I let you worm your way into my heart again."

"Sera." There was a warning in my tone. I wasn't sure if it was for her, or for myself.

She ignored it. With one hand on the wall, she carefully lifted one leg up and out of the tub. Slowly, she transferred her weight to that foot before lifting her other leg. I could see the lines of pain on her face, and it infuriated me that she wouldn't allow me to help her. No. Fuck that. Stepping beside her, I wrapped one arm around her waist just as her back gave out on her.

Without another word, she grudgingly allowed me to help her dry off and into my shirt. She didn't complain about wearing it. All of her clothes were still at Luigi's. And there was no way for us to get them without someone seeing and wondering why we needed them. I'd seen the clothes Veda loaned her on the bed, but I wanted her in mine. "Are you hungry? Do you need anything from downstairs?"

"No, I just want you to leave." She was right back to the way she was, as though nothing had happened.

"You don't mean that."

She looked me straight in the eye. "Yes," she said. "I do. I don't want anything to do with you, Enzo. And as soon as I can get the hell out of here, I'm leaving."

I stilled, but I didn't hide from her. I didn't try to disguise the pain her words brought. "And what if I don't let you go?"

"You have no choice," she informed me. "We made a deal. And you'll live up to your end of it, or I'll tell everyone what a lying son of a bitch you are and that your word means *nothing*."

Oh, I had a choice. And she was just going to have to live with it.

CHAPTER 9

Enzo

Sera had fallen asleep by the time I got the text that Tristan had returned. After I snuck into the bathroom and showered off the remainder of the blood, I put my sweats back on and added a T-shirt, then made my way down to Luca's office.

Tris was sitting on the couch with Luigi's phone in front of him, fingers typing away on the laptop he'd brought with him. His tie was lying beside him on the cushion and the first few buttons of his shirt were undone.

"Any progress?" I asked him.

"Getting there," he said.

Luca was standing over by the table where he kept his whiskey. He'd changed into a pair of jeans, a pullover cotton shirt, and some house shoes. He had a near empty glass in his hand. I joined him, pouring myself one.

"How is Sera?" he asked.

"Sleeping."

"Good." He finished what was in his glass in one swallow and turned to pour another. "Word of my father's death is getting around the family fast. I've already been contacted by Gino. He's setting up the meeting for tomorrow to vote in the new boss."

"So we need to find something tonight."

"Yes." He glanced over at Tristan as he took a sip of his whiskey. "My father was always careless about security. He was too confident of the power he wielded. Thought he was impervious to everything. Thought *no one would ever dare to try to take him down*." This was said in a perfect imitation of his father. "Hopefully, that'll play in our favor."

We chatted quietly about a few other things while Tristan worked on getting into Luigi's phone. It didn't take him long.

"I'm in."

Luca and I exchanged a look, then we joined Tristan in the sitting area in front of Luca's desk. Tristan tapped the phone screen a few times, then handed it over to Luca. Laying it flat on the table where we all could see, he went into his father's text messages and started to scroll.

Most had no name attached to them, just a phone number. He gave those numbers to Tristan if the wording, though innocent enough if anyone outside of the family saw it, seemed suspicious at all, who then looked them up on his laptop to identify the user. Whether or not they wanted to be found wasn't an issue. Tris would find them.

Then he moved onto the call list. I logged all of the numbers in the history into a notebook, noting times and dates of calls.

But the real winner came when Luca went into Luigi's saved voicemails. Specifically, one that was left on Luigi's wedding night, so he hadn't had a chance to listen to—or delete—it yet. Luca pulled it up and tapped the screen to put it on speaker. A man's voice, one we all recognized right away by the Boston accent, was loud and gruff in the quiet room.

"Hey, boss. Got your invitation to the fundraisah. I'll need a cah to pick me up at the airport, and I'll bring that gift to your son. It'll be mad quick. I won't get the chance to see everyone. But maybe next time, eh?"

Luca played it twice more, and then he set the phone down and leaned back on the couch, his expression unreadable. Tristan and I exchanged looks. That message may seem harmless to anyone who didn't know Boston Billy—the name of the hit man from the north end of Boston who was infamous in our world for being discreet, precise, and never getting caught. He was in and out. No muss. No fuss. Leaving dead bodies in his wake before anyone even realized he was in town.

Holy shit.

Luca's father had a hit out on him. And from the sound of it, he wanted Billy to take out me and Tristan too, but Billy decided it was too risky and it would have to be done at a different time. Smart move on his end. There was no fucking way he'd get to both of us before we found him.

Luca pulled his own cell phone out of the back pocket of his jeans and tapped in Billy's number. He didn't have to look at it. We all had it memorized. If any details needed to be discussed, he'd switch over to a burner phone and call from there.

"Billy." Luca sat forward and rested both elbows on his knees. "It's Luca. That gift you have for me? You can return it. Also, you should know, my father—Luigi—passed away tonight. Yeah. Thank you. No. No. Of course not. It's business. I understand. Yes. I'll let you know where you can send flowers. Give your wife my best. And have a Merry Christmas. Thank you." He hung up and laid his phone on the table beside his father's.

We wouldn't have to worry about Billy showing up at the fundraiser now. No one was alive to pay him.

When Luca just sat there, staring at the two phones lying side by side, Tristan spoke up. "This is an acceptable reason to have Luigi removed. It was your life or his. The family will accept it."

Luca nodded his head. "Yes. They will."

"And they will know I was the one who did it," I told him. "It would be expected."

"Yes," he said. "But there's no reason to name names. My father was a problem. He was taken care of. Just like my brother. End of discussion. We have the proof we need right here."

"It's enough for the family," Tristan said. "Very few will vote against you now. We know many stayed with your father out of fear, and now that that fear is gone, they have no reason to."

"Are you all right?" I asked my friend when he went quiet again.

"I will be," he responded. "By tomorrow, I will be." Clearing his throat, Luca grabbed his phone from the table and rose to his feet. "I'm going to bed. You both should do the same. I've doubled up the guards outside tonight, although I'm not expecting any problems. However, we may have to move again before all this is said and done."

"Or just purchase a second house in a secret location," Tristan said.

Luca smiled. Just a little, but it was there. "Or that."

We said our goodnights and went our separate ways to our rooms in Luca's large lake house. He was right. Tomorrow would be an eventful day. We needed to be alert. And hopefully, when all was said and done, Luca would be the head of the family. After all the hard work he's put in and all the shit he's taken from his family, he deserves it.

We just needed to live through tomorrow.

CHAPTER 10

Enzo

L uca offered to hold the meeting at noon in the upstairs room of his club, the same room we'd met Sera's father in, and the other members of the family agreed. More tables were brought up and drinks were supplied. Luca himself met the Capos at the elevator doors to shake their hands and welcome them. After they were checked for weapons, of course.

I stood just behind Luca, as did Tristan, and I received more than a few semi-hostile looks as men who'd known me since I was very young piled into the room. But I wasn't worried. Half of them had wanted to kill me for years for some of the things I'd done. After today, a few more wouldn't make that much of a difference.

When everyone had arrived, Tristan called the guards downstairs and told them to lock the doors to the club.

No one was to go in or out until a decision had been made.

I gave a nod to two of Luigi's men as they joined us at the big table. "Tony. Marco."

"Enzo." Marco returned the gesture as Tony glanced around the room. Marco was a long-time member of the family, of the older generation, and had been with Luigi for as long as I could remember. Tony was his son, and was still learning his manners. However, someday, he was going to piss off the wrong person, and they'd get beaten into him before his daddy could save him.

As Luca was still the underboss, and the only living son of the deceased, he was the first to speak. "As you all know by now, my father was killed last night," Luca announced to the room at large. Condolences were spoken, and he accepted them with the spirit in which they were given before turning his attention to the two men who'd been at Luigi's when it happened. "What were the police told?" he asked Marco.

"We told them what we always tell them. We have no idea what happened. The door was locked. We found him that way and his new bride was gone. No, we didn't see or hear anything. Etc. Etc."

"And any incriminating evidence was cleaned up before they arrived?"

They both nodded.

Luca nodded. "Good. As soon as they release his body, we'll start the funeral arrangements."

Marco stood up, and everyone's attention turned to him. Except for mine. I continued to scan the room for any signs of anyone who wanted to take the decision being made today into their own hands. "As the only living son and the underboss, it's the natural order of things that you, Luca, should be voted in as boss. But you know everyone's going to be thinking the same thing we are, so I just thought we should talk about the elephant in the room, so to speak. I'm not saying you did this, and I'm not saying you didn't. All I'm saying is that there will need to be proof that this wasn't just you getting tired of waiting, if you know what I mean."

"I do," Luca told him.

"Good," Marco said. "And please accept our condolences, also. Your father, like your brother, will be greatly missed."

"No," Luca said. "He won't. Luigi was a self-centered bastard who rose to his position strictly through intimidation and fear, and treated his men worse than dog shit on his shoe. He treated his family even worse. Me, in particular."

"With all due respect, Luca," Marco said. "You shouldn't speak ill of the dead like that."

Luca leveled an icy blue stare at him. "Why not?" When he didn't respond, Luca leaned back in his chair. "So you think I killed my father in a power play."

"Not you specifically, no," Tony answered. He didn't say anything more, or even so much as glance my way, but the implication was there that he knew exactly who'd pulled the trigger.

"Well," Luca told him. "I have a lot of respect for you, Marco. And I've always been honest with you, so I'm going to be honest with you now."

Pulling out his phone, he held it up for all to see. "I have a recording of a message left for my father. From Boston Billy." Tapping his phone screen, he played the message we found last night. When it was done, he slid his phone back into the inside pocket of his suit jacket. He didn't explain what the message meant. There was no reason to. Everyone there could interpret the true meaning behind it.

Luca turned to look at Marco and Tony. "I assume you two knew absolutely nothing about this?" he asked them.

Marco met his stare. "No. Of course not." But I could smell the sweat running down his spine. "It's a shame, what happened to your father," he told Luca. "A damn shame. May he rest in peace."

A few men made the sign of the cross. No one else asked any questions or made any other comments. The pieces of what happened the night before fell into place, and everyone would assume that Luca had done what he had to do to protect himself. No one would blame him.

One of Gino's sons spoke up from a table near the back corner. "What about Luigi's new wife?"

Turning my head, I stared at him through my sunglasses as adrenaline began to burn through my bloodstream. To keep myself from going for the gun I had strapped to my calf, I laced my fingers together on top of the table.

"What about her?" Luca asked.

"She's missing, ain't she?"

"Yes," Luca told him.

"She was staying with you for a while, is that right? Did she know about this?" he asked. "Because I'm thinking that maybe she was in on all of this, and it would be nice to know where she is now."

"Was she planted in your father's house by you?" Gino added.

Luca stared at him for a long moment, and I knew what he was thinking. How the hell did these guys know Sera was at Luca's house? Did Luigi tell them? Or her father? "My father's widow is completely innocent," he told them. "She knows nothing except that her wedding night was ruined."

"Then she's a witness," Gino said. "And now she's disappeared."

Marco turned to me. His eyes fell to my injured hand, and I flexed my fingers. "Do you have any idea where Serafina is?" he asked. "We know you two were...close."

I smiled, but it was cold. "I fucked her, Marco. More than once. That's it."

"She never mentioned anything to you? Nothing personal at all? Any friends in the area?"

"It was kind of hard for her to speak with my cock stuffed between her lips."

"Serafina will not be a problem," Luca told him.

"If she's a witness, then she needs to be dealt with."

The room came alive with murmured agreement.

Luca waited until things died down. "I'll deal with my father's widow. She won't be a problem. My guess would be she's not exactly heartbroken about the turn of events."

"But now she's a liability," Gino's son said. "She could be out there talking to the cops right now."

I couldn't keep my mouth shut anymore. "Sera won't talk."

Gino narrowed his eyes at me, his distrust of me clear to read. "How do you know? You just said you only used her to warm your dick."

I gritted my teeth at his disrespect, but I kept my tone even and controlled. "Because she grew up in this world.

And she's not stupid." I didn't have to say the rest, that she knew if she talked she'd be the next one taking a long nap in the dirt. "Besides..." I allowed my gaze to roam over the room, meeting the eyes of everyone there. "Luca said he'll handle her. So consider her handled." Even with my sunglasses on, most of the men fidgeted nervously when my attention was on them.

"Shall we move on?" Luca suggested. With a nod at Marco, he handed the floor over to him.

"All right," he said. "You all know how this works..."

The vote didn't take long, and Luca was officially put into the position of Boss. It was a close call, however, between him and Gino, and the latter wasn't taking the loss well, although he tried to put on a nonchalant face.

We talked about some other matters and agreed to meet there again after the holiday. Then the Capos were shown out to go spend time with their families—after all, it was Christmas day—while we waited to hear from the police that Luigi's body had been released.

When everyone was gone, I rubbed my eyes with my uninjured hand, trying to ease the ache behind them. But it was no use. "Whatever you feel you need to do to me, do it," I told Luca. "I deserve it. If you want to take me outside right now and put a bullet through the middle of the head, I won't try to run. All I ask is that you take care of Sera."

"I'm not going to kill you," he said after a pause. "Even though honor dictates that I should." He sighed heavily and ran a hand through his dark blond hair. "I hated my father. You know that."

"He was still your father."

But Luca only shook his head. "If you hadn't killed him, I would've done it myself eventually."

My eyes snapped up to his.

"You fucked up last night. Really fucked up. Not because you killed him, but because you were careless. Also, I don't have enough of the family on my side yet. At least not where I'm sure of their loyalty to me, and now we have to contain the damage." He paced away a few steps and back again, thinking.

"What about Sera?" I asked him. "She'll be killed on sight if anyone sees her before we can prove she won't rat on us. Even if they're loyal to you."

"Yes," he said. "But I'll do everything I can to help you keep her safe until things calm down."

My eyes met his, and I hoped my sincerity showed as I said, "Thank you, Luca."

"You don't have to thank me. You helped me with Veda when she first came here. You still do. And I know you would give your life for her. I will do the same for your Sera."

Though guilt still ate away at me for I'd done, I was humbled by the love and forgiveness of this man who was not only my friend, but my brother. Sometimes, it wasn't the blood in your veins that bound you and made you family, but the blood you were willing to spill for each other.

He suddenly smiled. "Take the rest of the night off and go see to your girl. Hell, maybe if you get her a nice enough present, you can convince her to like you again." With a smirk, he grabbed his jacket from the back of the chair where he'd laid it earlier and shrugged it on as we walked toward the elevator.

Sera was angry with me, and I didn't blame her. I'd be angry too if someone had done the same to me. And I wouldn't easily forgive them.

But now that I had her back, what was I going to do with her? It was quite obvious to me now that, much as I told myself I would forget her, there was no fucking way in hell I would be able to sit back and watch her marry someone else. The very idea of witnessing her walk down the aisle toward another man—again—gnawed away at my insides until I felt sick.

When I gave her up, I'd just kept telling myself that no matter what happened with her, it was better than ending up dead. Which is what would've happened if she'd stayed with me, and, like my previous wife, got on Luigi's radar somehow. Which honestly wouldn't be hard. Her pink hair alone would make her stand out. And if he'd noticed that she was special to me, he would've used her to get to me anytime he felt he needed to. Because that was the kind of bastard he was.

And when she became a thorn in his side, he would remove her permanently. But he wouldn't dirty his own hands. Oh, no. Doing it himself would put a target on his back, so he would make me do it. A test of my loyalty.

I wanted to think that I was better than that now. Stronger. But the god's honest truth was I didn't know what I would do if I was ever again put in the position of choosing between my only family and the woman I cared about.

So I did what I had to do to keep her safe, knowing she would hate me for it.

But now, Luigi was gone. Luca, my friend and brother, was the new boss. And I had faith in him. It was what he'd been groomed for. But he was also a man who understood what it was like to have a woman become the very air you breathe, and who would never order another man to do something so sick as to put a bullet into his own wife.

A sense of relief so strong it made me lightheaded rushed through me. No, I would never have to make that choice again. Sera could be mine forever.

I just had to talk her into forgiving me. And then keep her alive long enough to prove she wasn't a rat.

CHAPTER 11

Serafina

I didn't see Enzo for a week after the night he shot Luigi and took me back. When I asked Veda about it while we were going through some of her clothes she was letting me borrow until the stuff I'd ordered online came in, she told me as far as she knew he was out of town on business for Luca. I was surprised he'd left without telling me. But then again, the last time he saw me, I didn't exactly make him think I cared.

And I didn't...or, at least, that's what I kept telling myself.

My back was feeling a lot better. The welts had gone down and there were only a few red marks scattered across my right side and back of my hip where the belt had hit me the hardest. After that first night, Veda and Lisa had helped me when I needed them. By the third day, the pain was more tolerable, and I was able to do everything on my own. I tried to keep myself busy helping Veda take down the Christmas decorations, and not think about the man who had caused such an uproar in my life these last weeks. But it was impossible. No matter how much he'd hurt me, he'd also saved me. More than once.

Why would he do that if he didn't care?

He'd found me when no one else could. He'd killed for me. He'd shown up on my damn wedding night just to watch me through the window and make sure I was okay. And when I wasn't, he'd come smashing through the window like some kind of knight in dented armor to save me.

He'd *killed the mafia boss* to save me. Without a thought for himself or what could've happened to him.

But he'd also done some real asshole things that weren't so easily forgiven. And I wasn't sure that I wanted to, even if I could, because forgiving him would make it that much harder to leave him.

I was eating dinner at the table in the kitchen with Luca and Veda when Enzo returned from wherever the hell he went. As soon as he came into the room—dressed in his usual fitted black suit, black dress shirt, black shoes, tie, and sunglasses—every cell in my body went on alert like I was a vampire and his blood was the only thing that could sustain me. I felt starved for him. My mouth watered, and I was suddenly entirely too warm as my blood raced through my veins in anticipation, but I clenched my teeth together and returned my eyes to my plate.

Without a word, Enzo came to stand beside me. My skin prickled, all too aware of his nearness. I heard a crinkly sound and glanced over to find a plastic grocery bag in his hands I hadn't noticed when he walked in. Opening it up, he reached inside and grabbed something, then dropped it on the table beside my plate.

It was a human hand. The stump was still bloody.

My stomach heaved, and I shoved my chair back from the table as Veda slapped a hand over her mouth. Luca kept eating his dinner as though there wasn't a bloody body part on the table. As a matter of fact, when I looked at him for his reaction, he didn't seem surprised at all. "What the hell is that?" I asked Enzo.

Instead of answering me, he reached back into the bag and pulled out something else, dropping it beside the first one. It was another hand. Only this one wore a ring I recognized. It was the ring I'd stolen from one of the men who'd raped me in the house in Mexico. The ring I'd given to Enzo when I'd asked him to kill them for me, along with the money clip and the watch.

He dug around at the bottom of the bag and retrieved the last item, dropping it beside the two hands. "I took this first, while he was still alive. He screamed in terror until he lost his voice. I recorded it for you on my phone."

It took me a second to realize it was a shriveled-up penis.

"I've been hunting this man since you gave me his ring. I recognized the crest on it right away and knew where to find him, but somebody tipped him off that I was looking for him and he wasn't easy to chase down. I would've brought him to you alive, but it was too much of a risk. I didn't even have time to get rid of the body before I had to make a run for my plane and get the hell out of there. Luckily, I was prepared and didn't leave any evidence. I'm still working on the other two."

"You're sure you left no reason for the authorities to look this way?" Luca asked.

Without taking his eyes off me, Enzo nodded.

I was still staring at the penis in shock. "You've been hunting them?"

"I told you I would," he said simply. "I promised you I would kill the men who hurt you. And I keep my promises."

"Not always." Tearing my eyes away from the evidence of my revenge, I stared up at him, daring him to deny it.

"Why don't we go to the other room?" Veda said to Luca.

He must've agreed, for they gathered up their plates and drinks and left the room. Neither Enzo nor I even glanced their way.

"You promised me you would never give me back to my father, and then you handed me over to him like it was nothing. Like *I* was nothing." My voice broke.

With one hand, he took off his sunglasses and set them on the table. His dark eyes burned with bloodlust and sorrow. "I was *trying* to protect you."

I looked around the kitchen, searching for these invisible threats that were so dangerous to me. "From what, exactly?" I asked him. "You brought me here because it was safe. That's what you told me. So, what the hell did I need protecting from that would make it worth it to give me back to my father?"

Pulling out the chair to my left at the end of the table, he unbuttoned his jacket and sat down. "I told you." He sighed wearily and rubbed his eyes with the thumb and forefinger of one hand. "From me." A muscle twitched on his face, right above the scar from my father's bullet.

"I know what you told me. But if you're so damn worried about me, Enzo, then why do you keep forcing me to be with you? I don't want to be here. I don't want to be with you." Every word caused the ache in the center of my chest to grow sharper, but I wouldn't take them back. "So just let me go."

"I tried," he told me. He sounded angry. With me? Or with himself?

"Giving me back to the man I was trying so hard to get away from isn't giving me my freedom. What the hell were you thinking?"

"What was I thinking?" he repeated incredulously. And then his shoulders dropped, and he scrubbed his face with his hands before he said, "I thought if I gave you back to him, I would still know where you are. What was going on with your life. Whereas if I let you go..." he paused, and his eyes caught mine. "I would lose you."

"Well, your reasoning wasn't quite accurate." Standing up, I went to walk past him. "Because you've lost me anyway."

Fast as a striking snake, his hand whipped out and grabbed my wrist.

I glared down at the offending appendage, surprised when there wasn't a drop of blood on it. "Let go of me."

At first, he wouldn't look at me. His fingers tightened almost to the point of pain. When he finally did catch my gaze, the burning intensity in his eyes was such that it made me catch my breath and I almost took a step back. "What would you like me to do?" he asked softly. "Would you like me to beg? Get on my knees and swear my undying love and devotion to you?"

At the word "love," my heart skipped a beat. But I shoved down any empathy I felt for him. "There's nothing you can do, Enzo. It's too late. So let me go."

But instead of doing as I'd asked, he came out of his chair and fell onto his knees at my feet, his hands moving to my waist as he sat back on his heels. His fingers dug into my flesh. "I can*not* let you go," he said as his eyes roamed over my hips before dipping down between my legs. "I will never let you go again, Sera."

"I'll hate you if you force me to stay here. You know that."

He tipped his head back and looked up into my eyes, a crazy smile playing about his sensual mouth. "I don't care. You're mine, Sera. And I'll spend the rest of my life doing whatever I have to do to make you happy. I'll give you whatever you want."

"I *want* to be free of you." It wasn't true. I wanted to be free of the mafia. Free of this world. But I couldn't honestly say I wanted to be free of him. I didn't think I'd ever be completely free of Enzo, no matter how far I ran. I knew in my soul his eyes would haunt me forever.

"Except for that," he said. "I can't give you that."

"So, you'll keep me a prisoner?"

He shook his head. "I don't think it'll have to go that far." His eyes dropped back down to my body as his hands slid up my sides to cup my breasts. "I think you could learn to love me."

And that was just the thing. Despite everything he'd done to me, I think I already did.

I swayed toward him before I could catch myself, not knowing where to put my hands. I wanted to run my fingers through his spiky hair and pull his head toward me until I felt his mouth on my skin, but instead I kept my hands at my sides. They tightened into fists as he gripped my ass and pulled my hips forward.

"Mmmm." His face was between my legs, and he inhaled deep. "I love the way you smell."

A whimper formed in the back of my throat, and I choked it down.

"I love the way you taste even more," he continued. "There won't be a day that goes by that I don't taste you here."

I realized he was tugging on the waistband of the yoga pants I'd borrowed from Veda, along with the long-sleeved, red and white striped shirt I wore. It reminded me of a candy cane and probably looked great with her blonde hair. Not so much with my pink. But it was soft and it kept me warm. My hands flew to his as my eyes went to the open doorway where Lisa would probably walk in any minute. Or worse, Luca and Veda. "Stop. You have to stop."

"No." His lips were on my skin. He was too strong for me, and my pants came down easily until they were around my thighs. The muscles low in my belly clenched tight as his hands squeezed my hips. "You don't want me to stop."

He was right. My body gave absolutely no fucks at all about our past. And the fact that someone could walk in on us at any moment only excited it. I trembled with anticipation as his hands slid around to the front of my hips and his thumbs parted the folds of my pussy, exposing me to his hungry eyes. I was already so wet, and he'd barely fucking touched me.

"Spread your feet wider," he ordered, his eyes never leaving my pussy. "As much as you can."

Black dots danced in front of my eyes, and I sucked in a breath, then eased my feet as far apart as my pants would allow.

"Thank you." His voice was low and husky.

I cried out breathlessly as he leaned forward and tasted me, his tongue soft and wet and warm as it swirled around my clit... I'd never felt anything as good as his mouth on me. I allowed myself to enjoy it for a few seconds before I tried to push him away. But he only chuckled, the sound vibrating through me until, instead of trying to get him off of me, my fingers dragged through his spiky hair and gripped it tight.

My eyes closed and my legs shook as sweet tension tightened my inner muscles in waves of pleasure until the only thing keeping me upright was Enzo's strong hands. I knew I should force him to stop. To let me go. Someone could walk in here at any second. But honestly, I didn't want him to. I was close. So fucking close...

Suddenly, his mouth was gone, and cool air hit my exposed sex as his hair was ripped from my fingers. My hands flailed in the air and my eyes popped open, searching the room as my heart galloped in my chest. But no one was there. It was just us. I looked down. Enzo was watching me with eyes that were black with desire, his chest rising and falling with every quick breath, just like mine.

"Tell me you want to stay with me, and I'll make you come."

"That's not fair," I whispered.

"Say it," he ordered. He still held me with his big hands wrapped around my hips, his thumbs holding me open and exposed. As he waited for my response, he ran the pad of one thumb over the sensitive bundle of nerves of my clit. My hips jerked forward as a shock wave of near painful pleasure shot through me, and he smiled. "Tell me."

"It would be a lie." My voice was little more than a whisper.

"Would it?" he asked just as softly.

I stood there, wracked with need, but too damn stubborn to give him what he wanted to hear. "Yes."

"I don't believe you."

I tried to pull away from him, but he wouldn't let me go. "I don't give a shit what you believe. Let me go."

"No. Now tell me the truth, Sera. Tell me you want to stay with me."

My hands covered his and our gazes clashed. There was nothing but raw desperation in the dark depths, the truth he couldn't hide with his self-controlled attitude, and I nearly cried out at the power of it. Unable to speak, I just shook my head.

His jaw tightened, and with a growl of hunger, he found me again with his mouth.

CHAPTER 12

Enzo

The woman was too fucking stubborn for her own good. I gave up on my need to hear the words to have her taste back on my tongue. The musky sweetness of her arousal filled my nose and mouth, and my body responded in force. I groaned as my cock swelled impossibly hard.

This time, I was going to come inside of her.

I needed to get her upstairs. Right fucking now.

With one last lick of her swollen flesh, I rose to my feet, pulling her stretchy pants up as I went. Before she could start arguing with me again, I bent forward, lifting her off the floor and over my shoulder. I was careful about it, just in case her back still hurt. One hand on her sweet ass to hold her in place, I strode from the kitchen and headed toward the stairs that would take us upstairs to our room.

I felt her palms flat on my lower back as she braced herself for the ride, but other than that, she didn't struggle. Her mouth, however, wasn't so easily contained. "What the hell are you doing?"

"Taking you upstairs so I can fuck you without anyone walking in on us."

"I don't want to—"

I lifted my hand off her ass and brought it back down with a loud smack, effectively cutting off what she was about to say. Then I kneaded the soft flesh to ease the sting. We were at the top of the stairs now, and I hightailed it in the direction of our room.

Down below, Luca came from the hallway that led to the media room with his and Veda's empty plates in his hands. He looked up when he noticed me through the open rails of the banister, saw Sera thrown over my shoulder, shook his head, and kept going into the kitchen.

In our room, I closed the door behind us and locked it, then set Sera on her feet. I grabbed her face and brought her mouth to mine. I didn't want to hear any more of her bullshit. I fucked up. I fucked up hard. I knew that. But right now, I needed to be inside her, and no matter what she tried to tell me, she wanted it too. I could feel the way she responded to me. I could feel her lies. We could fight later. After I'd come inside of her so many times my balls were shriveled and purple and my cock was raw and neither one of us could walk.

I shrugged out of my jacket and left it lying on the floor where it landed. With one hand on the back of her neck so she couldn't pull away, I used the other one to rip open my shirt. Buttons flew and scattered across the floor. These clothes cost me an easy two grand, but I didn't give a fuck. I needed to feel her skin on mine.

My shirt joined my jacket, and I growled deep in my throat as Sera's teeth sank into my lower lip, drawing blood. I paused in my disrobing to shove my hand down the front of her pants. She was so wet my fingers easily slid between her folds and found her clit.

Sera moaned, her mouth going slack beneath my lips.

When her fingers were digging into my shoulders, I pulled my hand out and broke off the kiss so I could pull her shirt up over her head. It joined my clothes on the floor. She wasn't wearing a bra. I bent down and sucked one hard nipple into my mouth. Her back arched as she fed me more of her breast, and her moan of pleasure was the sweetest thing I'd ever heard.

Jesus Christ, she was so responsive to me. It made me fucking crazy. I needed to be inside of her. Everywhere. So she would have no doubt in her mind who she belonged to. When it came to her body, I would be her first for everything.

And her last.

Releasing her nipple, I picked her up with an arm beneath her ass and the other hand still holding the back of her neck. Her legs went around my waist and my cock pressed against her sex through our clothes. Her bare breasts pressed against my naked chest, and it felt so good, a shudder ran through me. In my arms, Sera did the same as her arms tightened around my neck.

It took forever to reach the bed. I laid her down on the white comforter and bent over her, taking her face between my palms and forcing her to look at me. "How is your back? Do you still have any pain? I don't want to hurt you."

"Just a little," she told me.

"Okay." I took her bottom lip between my teeth and sucked it into my mouth before releasing it. "You tell me if I get too rough."

She nodded, and I felt her fingernails dig into my sides, urging me to hurry.

I pulled off her sneakers, socks, and pants. My eyes never left her stunning face as she watched me take off the rest of my clothes, her heated gaze tracing the tattoos on my shoulder and pec before dropping down to the one above my hip. The next time I went to get some ink, I'd take her with me and brand her as mine for all to see. Just thinking about it caused a rush of blood from my head to my groin.

As soon as I was done getting undressed, I pulled her ass to the edge of the bed and spread her legs wide as I knelt on the carpet between them to finish what I'd started in the kitchen. With my thumbs, I spread her pussy wide. She was dark pink and swollen and glistening from my mouth and her own arousal. I wanted to make her come. Wanted to hear her cry out my name as her body bucked beneath my mouth. So that's what I did.

"Enzo!"

Fuck, yes.

One arm across her hips to hold her still, I slid two fingers deep inside of her, then began slowly sliding them in and out. With my tongue and teeth, I brought her to orgasm, her sweet pussy quivering under my mouth as she pulsed around my fingers. And I didn't let her go until she went limp. Only then did I set her back down on the bed and get to my feet.

Drops of come glistened on the head of my cock and I gripped myself in my hand, spreading them around before I lined myself up with her pussy. I slid inside just far enough to know I was where I wanted to be, and then I took her hips again and with one strong thrust I pushed my cock so deep inside of her my balls hit her ass.

She cried out as her body gripped me so tight it was almost painful. I'd never felt anything as fucking good as Sera wrapped around my cock. My heart pounded in my chest and sweat dripped down my temples, but I forced myself to hold still. "You okay, baby girl?"

Her bottom lip between her teeth, she nodded. My muscles trembled with the need to take her hard and fast. I moved, just a little, and watched as her eyes fluttered closed and her back arched with pleasure.

Ahhhh...Fuck *me*.

I clenched my jaw, and I tried, I really did, but I couldn't hold off anymore. So I dug my fingers into her hips and I fucked her the way I'd been dreaming about since I walked out of that room above Luca's club.

But it wasn't enough. I needed to break her. To mark her. To own her. To twist her up inside until she never tried to fucking leave me again. Until she was so ingrained as my own, the thought of my life without her was completely unfeasible to me. Until I was the only one she reached for when she needed to be fucked like this. Or when she needed comfort. Or anything at all. I would be the one she ran to. The one she fantasized about.

Only me.

With a groan, I pulled out of her sweet pussy and flipped her over onto her stomach, her legs hanging off the high bed and her gorgeous ass on display. I fucking loved her thicker curves. So much sexier to me than the women who lived up to the typical beauty standards of today. Not that there was anything wrong with thinner women. All women were beautiful in their own way. They just weren't my thing.

The welts on her back had faded down to just a few slashes of pink on her pale skin, and there was still some bruising that hadn't faded away yet. I bent over her and kissed every mark, smiling when chill bumps danced across her skin. I rolled my hips, sliding my stiff cock between the cheeks of her ass.

Sera stiffened when I prodded her there, and I leaned over her, resting most of my weight on one forearm as I held her down on the bed with my hand once again at the back of her neck. "I won't hurt you," I promised. "No more than I have to. But I told you once this was going to be mine, too. And I meant it."

"You won't fit." There was fear in her voice even as she squirmed on the bed, pushing her hips up to meet me.

"I will, baby. You just need to relax and trust me."

I was shaking with the effort it took not to drive into her virgin ass. But I would hurt her if I did that. And I didn't want to hurt her. Taking my cock in my free hand, I rubbed it through the folds of her pussy, lubricating myself and her. Blood pulsed through the thick veins of my cock and I gave it a squeeze before letting it go. Wetting my thumb in my mouth, I rimmed her ass, then pressed inside, just a little at a time, getting her used to the feel of me there. She moaned when I pulled my thumb out and pushed it in again, deeper this time. "I'll make you feel so fucking good, baby girl," I swore.

When she was loosened up a bit, I replaced my thumb with the head of my cock. But she was so fucking tight, I couldn't make any headway. "Stay right there," I ordered.

I reached over to the nightstand. There was lube in there that I sometimes used when I'd stay here overnight and needed to take the edge off with a quick handjob. I brought it back to the bed with me and poured some into my palm. Fisting my cock, I rubbed it all over, nearly coming in my own hand at just the thought of being inside her sweet ass.

Sera watched me from her place on the bed. There was still a glimmer of trepidation in her eyes, but there was also curiosity and whole hell of a lot of lust.

Dropping the bottle on the bed, I used what was left on my fingers to spread it around and inside her ass as much as I could. Then I lined up the head of my cock again and, slow and easy, started to push my way inside of her.

Sweat trickling down my temples, I watched her carefully as I pumped the head in and out, going a little deeper each time. "You need to relax, baby girl."

"It hurts," she whispered.

Reaching beneath my balls, I found her clit with my fingers, still slippery with lube.

"Oh! Oh, god." Soon she was lifting her ass and pressing her hips back to meet me.

I gritted my teeth and pressed my free hand to her lower back to hold her steady. "I'm almost there, baby. I'm almost in. Jesus, you feel so fucking good." My breath sawed in and out of my lungs and my heart was pounding hard. I clenched my jaw, trying like hell to wait, to make it good for her.

Her ass looked so good wrapped around the thick girth of my cock, and I was so fucking hard it hurt, but it was the best kind of pain. "Are you all right?" The words came out on a gasp of air.

In response to my question, she spread her feet wider and lifted onto her toes. Her fingers fisted the comforter and her back arched as I carefully thrust forward, making me slide deeper inside of her. I cursed softly and slid my thumb inside of her pussy as I doubled my efforts with my fingers on her clit.

"More," she moaned.

Slow and steady, I pulled all the way out, then quickly pushed back in, deeper this time. Sera cried out and her body pulsed around my cock and my thumb as she came.

That was all it took.

With both hands spreading her ass, I picked up my pace, fucking her with long, hard strokes until I was as deep as I could go. My back buckled as I came so fucking hard inside of her I thought my heart was gonna stop, and I barely caught myself on my arms as I fell forward, my hips jerking into her ass.

When it was over, I dropped my forehead to the smooth skin of her back and just tried to breathe. I was still inside of her and still half hard. Moving her hair aside, I kissed the back of her neck, tasting the salt on her damp skin before I whispered in her ear, "You belong to me, baby girl. Every fucking inch of you."

For once, she didn't argue with me.

CHAPTER 13

Serafina

Enzo kept me with him all night and half of the next day. The only reason we got out of bed was to shower or use the bathroom. He only left me once while I was dozing to bring us some wine and leftovers from dinner so I wouldn't be hungry.

And through it all, he reminded me who I belonged to, both with his words and his body, until I stopped trying to deny it. To deny him. And he was right. What was the point? I'd only be lying.

"Don't you have to work?" I asked him. He was wrapped around me, his front to my back, his cock still inside of me as he lazily stroked my hip and thigh.

He nuzzled my neck. "Tristan covered for me last night and today. But I'll need to go out tonight."

"What's happening tonight?" As soon as I asked, I remembered who I was talking to. Twisting around as much as I could, I looked over my shoulder at him. "Sorry. You don't have to tell me."

His dark eyes burned into mine, and my heart skipped a beat. He always made me feel like every time he looked at me was the first time. And those eyes told me quite clearly how I affected him, even when he couldn't find the words. "There's a holiday fundraiser tonight that Luca needs to go to," he told me as he gently brushed a strand of my hair away from my eye. "I always go with him, as does Tristan. It would be strange if I wasn't there. People might get suspicious, so I need to go."

"Is Veda going?"

"Mmhmm," he said distractedly. "Dates are required. Otherwise, it would just look like a big meeting of mob bosses to the outsiders who will be there, which is exactly what it is. Deals will be discussed, new partnerships made, grievances aired, etc. All in hidden corners with secret handshakes." He smirked.

I turned my back to him again, not liking the possessive heat rising into my chest and face. Before I could stop myself, and knowing I wouldn't like the answer, I asked him, "Do you and Tristan have to take dates?"

He hesitated. "Yes."

Tears pricked my eyes, the strength of my spiraling emotions surprising me. I cleared my throat, and my voice was surprisingly steady when I asked the obvious follow-up question, "Who are you taking?"

"Sera..."

"I want to know."

"It doesn't matter."

I snapped my mouth shut. Even knowing it wasn't possible right now, somewhere deep inside, I was really hoping he would say that girl would be me. "I need to take a shower." I had to get out of that bed and away from him before he saw how crazy it made me to think of him with another woman.

"Hey." He stopped me as I tried to pull away from him and pulled me back into the warmth of his body. "It doesn't matter who I take. It's only for show."

"I know." I wouldn't look at him. I couldn't. If I did, I'd burst into tears. Taking the sheet with me, I scooted off the bed.

"Sera, don't be like this."

The gaping hole in my chest suddenly filled with rage. I spun around to face him. "Don't be like what?" I snapped.

He sat up on the bed, and I couldn't stop myself from admiring the picture he made. He was one of the most beautiful males I'd ever seen. All muscle and tats and hard lines and fierce dark eyes. Even though I was sore from being thoroughly used in every way he could imagine, just looking at him made my heart race inside of my chest and my thighs squeeze together.

"Don't do that. It doesn't matter who I'm taking tonight."

"Maybe it matters to me."

He didn't respond.

"It's Jade, isn't it? You're taking Jade." The fact that he was taking my friend didn't make me feel any better. She was an escort who fucked for money. There would be no feelings involved, except for mine. "Are you going to fuck her?" Then I shook my head. "Never mind. I don't want to know."

Before I could make a complete fool of myself, I turned on my heel and walked into the bathroom, shutting and locking the door behind me.

I'd just turned on the water for the shower when there was a knock on the door. "Sera. Open the door and talk to me."

I ignored him. I didn't want to talk to him right now. I wanted to get into this hot shower and feel sorry for myself for being such an idiot that I ever allowed myself to fall for this man at all.

"Sera. Open the fucking door. I'm not going to tell you again."

Barely holding back a sob, I turned to get into the shower just as the bathroom door flew open and smashed into the wall behind it. I jumped and nearly fell on my ass as my foot stepped on the sheet. My free arm flew out to catch myself, but there was nothing there.

Enzo, naked as the day he was born, grabbed my arm to steady me. With the other, he opened the shower door, reached in, and shut off the water. "Don't do that," he growled. "Don't shut me out. If something is upsetting you, I want to know what it is, even if it's me. So talk to me."

"There's nothing to talk about," I told him. "And even if there was, I don't want to." I was being a bitch. I knew that. But it was because I was hurt. And because I was used to holding my feelings inside, where it was safe. Growing up the way I had, showing any emotion only brought more attention to myself, and I learned really fast that that was the last thing I wanted to do. So, instead, I bottled it all inside of me and stole things as a way to refocus my anxiety, or something like that.

Enzo, however, did not agree with this coping mechanism. "I know you don't, but you're going to." Gripping my jaw, he forced me to look at him. I pressed my lips together and stared up at him rebelliously until he sighed. "I'm not going to fuck her."

"You don't seem very happy about that." I pulled my chin from his hand and his arm fell back down to his side. "Do what you want, Enzo. It doesn't matter."

He cocked his head to the side and narrowed his eyes. "How the hell could you even think such a thing after last night?"

I rolled my eyes. "Please. I know what kind of man you are."

He rested his hands on his bare hips, his cock half hard. "Yeah? What kind is that?"

This time, I didn't hesitate. "You're a mobster. You're a man who likes having power. You'll fuck who you want, whenever you want. And as soon as you get tired of me, you'll hide me away in a house somewhere while you flaunt your latest mistress in front of all of your buddies."

His eyes traveled over my pink hair, down to my eyes and nose with the silver nose ring, and then down to my lips. "How could I ever get tired of you, Sera?"

I pushed down the thrill his words brought. It would be stupid of me to let a few pretty phrases make me forget who and what he was. "I don't want you to go," I whispered.

The tension fell from his broad shoulders. "I have to, baby."

"Then take me."

But he was already shaking his head. "I can't. You know that."

"Can't? Or don't want to?"

"Sera..."

I was suddenly angry again. "DON'T 'Sera' me."

"I can't take you," he said. "You know I can't. It's too dangerous."

"Fine." Sarcasm dripped from my tone. I was done with this conversation. So I went back into the bedroom and started gathering up my clothes.

Enzo followed me out, and apparently, his patience was at an end. "I'm trying to keep you SAFE! Goddammit, Sera!" He stopped a few feet away from me, and there was pain in his voice when he said, "I can't lose you again."

I stopped trying to pick my clothes up off the floor. I couldn't hide the tears that slid down my cheeks. "You didn't lose me, Enzo. You *gave me away*."

I saw the truth in his eyes. He didn't even try to deny it this time. "Sera..."

"No. Just...stop."

Hands low on his naked hips, he stared at me. After a few tense moments, he said in a tone that would brook no argument, "I'm sorry. I can't take you. A few trusted guards will be here at the house to protect you while we're gone. If you're smart, you'll stay inside this time until everyone knows you're not going to rat on anyone to the cops about Luigi's murder." He paused. "I can ask Lisa to stay and keep you company."

"That's not necessary."

He looked like he wanted to say more, but then he just turned away and walked into the bathroom. A few seconds later, I heard the shower come back on.

The clothes I held fell out of my hand. Walking over to the bed, I sat down on the edge and stared at the floor as silent sobs wracked my body. I hated this. Hated feeling like this. I wanted to get away, start a new life far from him and this stupid life. And what I hated most was that I didn't hate him at all.

By the time Enzo finished his shower, I was dressed and downstairs in the media room. I didn't want to see him when he left. Didn't want to know how good he smelled or how amazing he looked, knowing he'd done all of that for another woman. I told myself it didn't matter. I didn't really care what he did. It was only my ego that was bruised. Besides, I was only going to stay here until it was safe for me to leave. As soon as I was able, I would demand my savings from Enzo and I would get the hell out of here. I'd go to Luca if I had to. And then I would start a new life where no one knew I was a mafia princess. I would change my name. Change my look. And I would become a whole new person.

I would forget this dangerous man that made my heart flutter inside my chest and every nerve ending come alive just by walking into a room, who risked his life for me only to push me away. I was tired of his indecisiveness. I didn't need him. I only needed myself.

I was curled up in one of the lounge chairs, paying absolutely no attention at all to the movie I'd thrown on the large screen when Enzo found me. Hands in the front pockets of his black dress slacks, he came to stand beside me. Without a word, he held out his hand.

Refusing to look at him, I took his watch off of my arm and dropped it into his open palm.

"Thank you," he said. "I'll be back as soon as I can." He didn't try to touch me or say anything else. He just...left... as I quietly cried.

CHAPTER 14

Serafina

I waited until everyone had gone before I threw off the blanket I'd pulled over myself and climbed out of the chair with the intention of taking a quick shower, drowning my sorrows in whatever alcohol and fattening food I could find, and watching a movie until I fell asleep. But my feet didn't move. Instead, I stood there for a minute as I stared at the closed door of the media room, my face hot with emotions I didn't want to name, until I was forced to drop all pretenses of being any kind of okay with the fact that Jade was spending the evening with Enzo instead of me.

For a moment, I was unsure of what I wanted to do. Scream? Cry? Trash Enzo's room?

I sank back down onto the chair. What the hell was wrong with me? I should be glad she was with him tonight. Maybe, after seeing her again, he'd remember how gorgeous and charming and fucking perfect she was and he'd forget all about me. After all, that was what I wanted. Right?

Right?

Staring off in the direction of the big screen without really seeing anything, I brushed away the tear that escaped and slid down my cheek.

It was what I *should* want. But somehow, even after all the shit he'd done, I couldn't seem to convince myself of it. I should forget about the money he stole from me and the stuff he offered me, take whatever I could steal, and get the hell out of this city. Leave Austin. Go somewhere else. Keep moving around. It would be the smart thing to do. By now, my father had to know that Luigi was dead, and he'd be furious that I'd fucked things up for him. Again. He would demand retribution, if he hadn't already.

Besides, I'd known when I stopped here that I wouldn't be able to stay long, and my original plan had been exactly that—make enough money for some food and gas and a place to live, then get back on the road. But with the discretion of the club, I'd stupidly thought I could stay for a few weeks, maybe even a couple of months before I'd have to run again. I made good money, and it would've provided me with enough to be able to get a really good head start. Plus, I'd thought that by hiding in plain sight, maybe I'd get away with it.

I realized now that I'd been naive. It was pure luck on my part that Enzo was the one on the other side of the door that night. Anyone else would've been on the phone to my father the moment word got out. I wiped at the moisture on my cheeks again. There were enough expensive things in this house that I could easily sell or pawn. If I was careful about budgeting my money, I should be okay.

Then why was I still sitting here?

Hauling my sorry ass to my feet, I made my way back upstairs, went into Enzo's room, and started the shower. I washed quickly and even blew dry my hair. Then I stared at myself in the mirror for a long time, contemplating what I was about to do. I needed to leave. And I would. But would it be so terrible if I saw him one more time before I did? And maybe by seeing him with Jade, it would give me enough of a shove to actually do it.

Lifting my chin, and wrapped only in a towel, I left the bedroom and went to the opposite end of the hall where Luca and Veda's room was.

I didn't even hesitate as I walked past the bed and into the en suite bathroom. I started opening drawers until I found Veda's makeup bag in the top right drawer next to the sink. Pulling it out, I found some colors that would look good on me and proceeded to make myself look like I hadn't been crying for the last few hours.

Once I was done, I went into the large walk-in closet. Veda's clothes hung on one side and Luca's on the other. A dresser with both of their things in it took up a part of one wall and their shoes took up the other. I stood there, staring at what that closet represented. Two lives coming together. Shared love. Acceptance.

An envelope lying on top of the dresser caught my eye. It looked like an invitation. Picking it up, I opened the envelope and slid out the piece of thick stock paper from inside. It was the invitation to the fundraiser tonight. Taking a deep breath, I put it back in the envelope and placed it back on the dresser, then walked in deeper and dug around in the back for a dress Veda most likely hadn't worn in a while. She had a lot of dresses. Apparently, Luca liked to take her shopping.

I found one that looked like it might fit my larger breasts, a gorgeous crimson gown that was little more than a full-length, satiny slip with tiny spaghetti straps, a low cut back, and a high slit in the skirt. I don't know why it was in the back. The dress was gorgeous and probably cost more than I'd made in a month.

The red would clash horribly with my pink hair, and that was the exact reason I'd chosen it. First, I'd be wearing a blonde wig, and I knew just the place to get one on my way to the fundraiser. Second, no one would expect a girl in hiding to show up at party wearing something as eye-catching as this.

Especially not a party full of the very people she was trying so hard to avoid.

Twenty minutes later, I was back in Enzo's room. I double-checked my appearance in the mirror behind the bedroom door. I'd taken the nose ring out of my nose and left it on the bathroom sink. Between that, the wig I'd use to cover my hair, and the heavy makeup I was wearing, I thought I'd succeeded in at least making it so no one would recognize me right off. And by the time they figured it out, hopefully I'd be gone, and they would be left wondering if it had really been me before blowing it off as a trick of the lighting.

I slipped into a pair of black heels, grabbed Veda's nice black jacket and clutch purse, and made my way downstairs.

This was the tricky part.

I had no phone. It was still at Luigi's with the rest of my things. So sneaking down the drive and calling an Uber was out of the question. Not that I would make it that far without someone spotting me anyway. So my only choice was to fake it until I made it. Enzo had told me when he'd first brought me here that no one knew I was here except the people inside the house. Not even the guards who patrolled the grounds. And I was going to use that to my advantage.

Throwing my shoulders back, I opened the front door and walked outside, shutting the door behind me and looking around. There was a guard standing at the bottom of the steps holding an automatic weapon, and he immediately turned around when he heard me come out, gun pointed at the center of my chest. Upon seeing it was me, he lowered it.

"Where's my car?" I asked him before he could question me. "It's supposed to be waiting for me."

He narrowed his eyes. "I wasn't told you were here, or anything about a car."

"Well, please have one brought around. Or call me an Uber, or whatever. Enzo is waiting for me at the fundraiser."

"Why wouldn't you have left with him?"

I tilted my head at him and pulled on my haughtiest mafia princess attitude. "Because I wasn't ready yet and I told him I would meet him there. Now are you going to get a car for me, or should I go back in that house and call Enzo and explain to him why I'm not coming?"

He stood in silence for a minute, chewing on the inside of his cheek, until finally he pulled his phone out of his inside jacket pocket. "I'll just call Enzo and see what's going on."

Fuck.

I kept the look of annoyed impatience on my face as he tapped the screen of his phone, then brought it to his ear. After a few seconds, he hung up without saying anything and went back to tapping, I assume to send him a text.

After another few minutes and no reply from Enzo, he finally called for a car. I didn't want to think about why he wouldn't be answering his phone, and firmly pushed it from my mind.

As soon as the Uber pulled up, I ran down the steps and hopped inside. "Drive. NOW!"

The driver, a young guy with black hair and a blue coat, took one look at the guard heading toward his car and stomped on the gas. "What the fuck?" he yelled, looking at me in the rearview mirror.

"That was just my brother," I told him with a roll of my eyes. "Don't worry about it."

He didn't seem too sure as he sped out of the open gate and onto the road, but he relaxed when it closed behind us, and he saw no one was following. It was what I had bet on. The guard wouldn't have called me an Uber if there were any vehicles left at the house.

It took us about fifty minutes and one stop at the club where I used to work to get there. One of the other girls who worked there often wore a blonde wig as part of her getup, and she always had a few stashed in her cubby in the break room. I was able to walk right in through the back door and out again with the wig without anyone being the wiser, since my security guy no longer had any need to be there. Within four minutes, I was back in the

Uber and on my way to the fundraiser as I pinned up my pink hair with the bobby-pins in my clutch and put on the wig.

I almost had the driver turn around at least eight times. What I was doing was dangerous and stupid and would probably end with me back at Luca's. Or possibly with a bullet through my head if someone else recognized me first.

Even knowing all of this, I couldn't bring myself to stop the chain of events I was about to unfold. Because the one thing that was worse than any of that would be to just sit back at Luca's house wondering if he was fucking Jade yet.

CHAPTER 15

Serafina

The fundraiser was in The Eleanor, an upscale event venue in the middle of downtown Austin. My Uber driver pulled up in front of the two-story black building squeezed between two multi-story buildings on 5th street. There was a small round sign jutting out from the building with the name of the venue. I thanked him and carefully got out of the car, then walked up to the double glass doors.

I stood on the sidewalk, staring at my reflection as the Uber pulled away behind me. My heart was beating so hard I thought it was going to burst right through my rib cage, and again, I wondered what the hell was wrong with me and what I was doing there. But before I could change my mind, the door was opened from the inside and I was greeted by a doorman in a black tuxedo.

"Welcome, madam. Do you have your invitation to the party?"

Shit. I should've grabbed Luca and Veda's. Would he have known it wasn't mine? Probably. I made a show of looking in my clutch purse. "Oh, no," I murmured. One hand still in my clutch, I looked off in the direction my driver went. "I must've left it in the Uber." I gave the doorman an apologetic glance. "Let me see if I can call him back."

He seemed content to wait, but fate was on my side because it chose that moment to start raining. Just a few fat drops here and there at first, but anyone who'd lived in Texas for any amount of time knows that those drops were your one and only warning that you have about ten seconds to find some shelter before the near hurricane level downpour hits you, soaking you through in a matter of point five seconds. And there was no awning or anything on the front of this building. It was only about forty degrees, and if he turned me away, I wasn't looking forward to freezing my ass off out here.

It only took one look of supplication from me for him to glance at the sky—even though it was too dark to see any rain clouds—and to wave me inside. "Don't worry about it," he told me. "I'm sure a lovely lady like you wouldn't have gotten all dressed up for nothing. May I take your coat?"

I glanced around. The room was made up entirely of shades of dark umber—the cement floors, the wood slat walls, and even the ceiling—lit up by sparkling pendant lights over the bar and large sconces along the walls. Even the benches and tables were a rich, dark brown, but from what I could see of the bar between the crowd, it was a creamy white with a dark top. I turned my back to the room and allowed him to help me remove my coat. He gave it to a younger man who'd been waiting behind him and then handed me a ticket, which I put in my clutch purse. "When you're ready to leave, just come back here and I'll fetch your coat for you."

"Thank you," I told him with a smile. We both glanced out the doors as the rain began to come down in earnest.

He turned back to me with a smile. "You're very welcome. Enjoy your evening."

I could feel the high testosterone level in the room. It hung in the air like a heavy fog. Apparently, you could take the man out of Italy, but you couldn't take the Italian out of the man. Letting one side of my straight blonde wig fall partially over my face, I turned to face the lions and walked into the room with long, sure strides. I felt numerous sets of eyes upon me, some of male interest, even more of female envy, but I didn't stop as I worked my way through the crowd, brushing past more men in tuxedos and women in their fanciest gowns. I just kept walking as though I knew exactly where I was going...

Because Enzo and Jade were standing at the bar in the front lounge.

Jade's back was to me, but even from this angle, I could see how stunning she looked in her backless, shimmery gold dress that fell just above her knees and showed off her gorgeous golden skin. The silky material clung to her perfect figure in all the right places, and I suddenly felt like a stuffed sausage the way my plump curves filled out my own dress. Her legs were bare, and her feet were in scrappy gold heels.

Enzo stood beside her, his head bent down to hers, one hand on her lower back above the material of her dress. I watched from the corner of my eye as his thumb caressed her bare skin. My stomach knotted as fire flashed through my blood, heating my face. I wanted to grab my friend by her shiny black hair and rip her away from him, then smash his damn sunglasses with my fist hitting his face.

But I did neither of those things. I did no more than give them a passing glance as I continued down the hallway and into the main room, where a small orchestra was playing pretty instrumental music. I kept walking until I reached the stairs at the back of the building and climbed them to find myself on the mezzanine level. Stopping at the bar, I ordered something in a martini glass made mostly of tequila and walked out onto the balcony. The couches were occupied, so I found an empty corner by the railing where I could look down over the main room. A few couples had started dancing to a version of a Halsey song and I sipped my drink as I watched them and tried to calm myself down.

But the longer I stood there, the more I wondered what I'd hoped to accomplish with this stunt. Why I was torturing myself like this. Standing here all night and watching Enzo with another woman, even if that woman was the only real friend I'd had in this town, would accomplish nothing but make me feel like shit about myself.

And what was I going to do when they left? Follow them like some kind of crazy girlfriend? Bust in after them and then freak out when I caught them in bed together? How many times had he brought her back to his hotel before he'd met me? I had no claims on Enzo. I didn't *want* to have any claims on him. The only thing I wanted was to get away from him and this world of fucking men who thought women were nothing but bargaining tools or playthings. Men who thought they could blackmail you and get away with it. So, what the hell was I still doing here? I'd seen what I'd come to see.

That was a good question.

I needed to leave. I shouldn't be here. Just because I didn't recognize anyone didn't mean that one of these assholes didn't know my father or hadn't seen my picture. And sooner or later, my luck was going to run out.

Yet I couldn't stop myself from searching the crowd below me for a glimpse of spiky dark hair and a hard jaw, eyes hidden by dark sunglasses so no one could see the fire behind them that I knew so intimately. When I didn't see him, I slammed down the rest of my drink and set my glass on a shelf set into the wall beside me. This was stupid. I needed to get the hell out of here and stop torturing myself. Fuck this. I was going to walk to the nearest bus stop, steal a wallet or some cash or something, and get the hell out of this city instead of just waiting around for someone else to decide how my life was going to go. Enzo could keep my fucking money. And I'd pay back the person I stole from the first chance I got.

I ignored the pain in my chest and the longing in my soul as I gave the room one more good search, telling myself it was only to get their location so I could make sure they didn't see me leave. I didn't see Enzo or Jade, so I could only assume they were still at the bar. Lifting my chin, because I was fucking better than this, I turned away from the railing...

"What the fuck are you doing here, Sera?"

His soft tone couldn't contain the rage seething beneath his calm words. My eyes widened as I came face to face with Enzo. Unable to help myself, they skittered down his body and back again. He'd added a black tuxedo jacket with a vest underneath to the black slacks and black dress shirt I'd seen earlier. Instead of a bowtie, he wore a satiny, narrow black tie. His pants showed off his muscular legs perfectly, and his shoes were buffed to a shine. My breaths sped up with my heartbeat and I felt my stomach tighten at the sight of him. "How did you know I was here?" It was the first thing I could think of to say.

He took a step closer, forcing me to take a step back and to the side until the railing was at my back and his big body completely hid me from view of the people behind him. Even in my heels, I barely came up to his chin. "Did you think your little disguise would hide you from me?" His eyes dropped to my breasts, then lower to my hips. My nipples hardened, and the silky material of the dress felt scratchy compared to the wet heat of his tongue that I longed for. "Did you think I wouldn't know the way you walk and the sexy curves of that ass?" He frowned as his chin lifted and I could feel his eyes traveling over my face and hair. "I fucking hate that blonde wig," he informed me.

With the way his mouth was twisted in disgust, I half expected him to rip it from my head and expose me to everyone there. "Jade wears wigs all the time." The words left my mouth before I could stop them.

He cocked his head to the side. "I couldn't tell you if Jade has ever worn one around me. I've never paid that much attention to her."

"That's not what it looked like when I got here. I saw you at the bar. It looked like you were paying quite a *lot* of attention to her."

He didn't feed my jealousy or try to explain his way out of it, which only pissed me off more. "So I take it you somehow talked the guards into letting you leave Luca's. And yet, instead of running—like you keep telling me is the only thing you want to do—you come here. Tell me why."

I dropped my eyes. I couldn't look at him. "Because I wanted to see."

Hooking his finger under my chin, he brought my eyes back up to his. "Wanted to see what?"

I tried to see his eyes behind the dark lenses of his glasses. "I wanted to see you with her," I said after a pause.

He stroked my cheek with the back of his fingers. "Why?"

It took me a moment to respond. "Because I thought if I did, I would stop wanting you."

"And did it work?"

I shook my head as tears of self-pity filled my eyes. I wanted to lie. To spew my jealous rage into his knowing expression. But I couldn't. All I could do was admit the truth. "No."

He brushed my cheek with the back of his knuckles, down my throat to the center of my chest, following the curve of one breast until the material of the dress stopped him. "No," he repeated softly.

The electricity that always crackled between us grew stronger. I wished I could see his eyes. "Where is Jade?"

"I put her in a cab."

"Why?"

"Because I don't want her," he told me. "I want you."

One tear escaped to slip down my cheek, and he brushed it away. "But I saw you whispering in her ear," I told him. "Saw you touching her back. Like you do to me."

"Not like I do to you."

"What's the difference?"

"I touch you like that because I can't *not* touch you, Sera. If I was touching her, it was just..." he paused, searching for the right word, "...habit."

I sucked in a shaky breath.

The tip of his finger followed the neckline of the red dress. "All I can think about right now is getting you out of this dress and being inside of you. I don't even remember what Jade was wearing."

"It was a gold—"

He cut me off. "I don't care." Glancing around my arm to the floor below, his brows came together in a frown. "Come on. I'm taking you out of here before you get us both killed, because if I see one more *stronzo* down there eating you alive with his eyes, I'm going to lose my shit."

My heart stopped, and I dug the narrow heels of my shoes into the floor as he reached for my hand and started to drag me away. "No, please!" I whispered loudly. "Enzo, wait!"

I didn't think he would stop, but he did. His jaw clenched so tight I could see the muscles pop out on the sides of his jaw, he waited.

"I can't go back there," I told him. "I can't go back to the lake house. Please," I begged. "I'm sorry I came here. I really am. But I was about to leave anyway." I paused, gathering my courage. "You can keep the money. You've taken what you wanted from me. Just let me go and I'll be out of the city by morning. No one will ever find me."

The corners of his mouth lifted in an evil smile. "Oh, baby girl. But I'm not finished with you. We're just getting started."

CHAPTER 16

Enzo

When I saw Sera walk into the fundraiser just as cocky as you please, I couldn't believe my fucking eyes. What the hell was she thinking? That a mangy blonde wig would hide her from me?

Like an animal, I could scent her the moment she walked into a room. Nothing she did or wore would keep me from knowing she was there.

I watched her in my peripheral until she disappeared from sight, not wanting to draw attention to her. I *watched* as every goddamn male in the place fucked her with his eyes until it was all I could do not to pull out my gun and start popping them off one by one just for daring to think of her that way. I wanted to shove my way through the crowd around the bar and shield her with my body—much as I was doing now—until I could get her the hell out of there, and it took every ounce of self-control I had to make my excuses to Jade and put her in a cab before I prowled the place room by room until I found her.

And yet, she was still trying to convince herself that she could leave me.

That I would just let her go.

I glanced over my shoulder, taking in the room and everyone within it. "We need to go. Now stop arguing with me and walk with me out of this venue. Calmly. Do not make eye contact with anyone. Do not say anything. Do not draw attention to yourself." I waited only long enough to make sure she was going to follow directions before I turned and started making my way through the crowd, pulling Serafina behind me.

I found Tristan in the main room where the actual fundraising was about to start with an auction, keeping a close eye on Luca and Veda as they stood in a corner of the room talking to Luca's uncle. "I need to leave. I have an...issue. Can you handle this yourself?"

Tristan glanced past me to where Serafina was standing quietly, her hand tightly gripped in mine. If he was surprised to see her, he didn't show it. "I'll explain to Luca."

"Thank you. I'll check in with you later tonight." I wasn't taking Sera back to Luca's. Not immediately. And not because she'd asked me not to.

I wasn't taking her there because seeing her walk across the floor in that slip of a dress, every curve and dip of her body on prominent display, had set my blood on fire. And when I'd found her upstairs, it was all I could do not to bend her over the railing and throw the skirt of that damn dress over her head. However, the danger to her was very real, and it was the only thing that kept me from fucking her senseless in front of all of these people, but the pure lust raging through me wasn't going to wait for us to drive all the way back to Luca's. I was taking her back to my hotel room. It would be safe enough for a few hours. Tomorrow, we would return to the lake house.

The door man gave her a warm smile as we collected her coat. "I see you found your gentleman," he said.

Sera gave me a nervous glance. "I did. Thank you so much."

"Take good care of her now." He smiled at me, and I bared my teeth at him in response. With a lift of his eyebrow, he held the door open for us. "At least the rain has stopped. Have a good evening!"

With my arm around her shoulder, I hustled Sera out into the damp, cold air and gave the valet my ticket. A few minutes later, he pulled the SUV up to the curb and hopped out. I helped Sera inside and gave him a healthy tip, then scanned the area around us as I walked around the front of the vehicle and got into the driver's side.

"Enzo, I—"

Grabbing her by the back of her neck with one hand, I yanked her over to me, my mouth crashing down on hers. She tasted like tequila and disobedience, and she made me fucking crazy. I wanted to rip the stupid wig from her head and pull her onto my lap and fuck her right there on the street.

With every ragged breath I took, her scent filled my lungs. Her moans filled my ears. Her taste filled my mouth. I was surrounded by Sera until I couldn't escape. And I was beginning to realize that I didn't fucking want to.

I released her as suddenly as I'd kissed her. "Put your fucking seatbelt on and give me your bag."

She blinked at me, her eyes unfocused and her chest heaving. "What?" she asked breathlessly. "Why?"

"Give it to me." I held out my hand.

She dropped the small black purse into my hand and pulled her seatbelt across her body with shaky hands.

I opened the bag. It held some bobby pins and a twenty-dollar bill. "Is this your money?"

"No."

"Where did you get it?"

She searched the interior of the SUV. "I think it was just lying on a table."

I left it where it was, closed the purse, and handed it back to her.

"Where are we going?" she asked me when I pulled away from the curb.

"To the hotel."

I felt her eyes on my face.

"What?"

"Nothing," she whispered as she turned away.

The short drive did nothing to calm me down. When we arrived at the hotel, I helped Sera unbuckle her seatbelt and pulled her out of the driver's side. I wasn't taking any chances that she'd try to get away from me. Tossing my keys to the valet, I held her tight to my side as we crossed the lobby to the elevators.

As soon as we were inside and the doors slid shut, I had her up against the wall. One hand held her wrists above her head as the other one started pulling up her skirt. My mouth slanted across hers, taking her lips in a brutal kiss. It didn't matter that I'd just fucked her more times than I could count only hours before. My body burned for her, every cell of my body screaming to be inside of her. I wanted to crawl under her skin, to feel her surround me until there was nothing but her and I.

The elevator door dinged as it slid open. With a growl of frustration, I released her and let her skirt drop. Taking her wrist, I led her to the door to my room and took her inside.

She spun around to face me, her eyes wide. Her lips swollen from my kisses.

"Take off that damn wig," I ordered as I locked the door.

"Enzo—"

"Take it off."

Slowly, too slowly, she reached up and took it off. Her pink hair was pinned close to her head.

"Take your hair down."

I took off my jacket, watching her as she looked around, then laid the wig and her purse down on the side table. She took off her jacket and hung it on the hanger. One by one, she pulled the pins from her hair until it fell in a wavy pink waterfall around her perfect face.

I pulled off my tie and took off my vest, laying them both over my arm with my jacket. "Go into the bedroom," I told her, my patience growing thinner by the second. "Go. Now."

She stumbled a bit as she turned away and walked in front of me to the bedroom.

I threw my coat, vest, and tie into the chair in the corner. "Take off the dress, Sera."

Without pause, she slid the dress from her shoulders, leaving them bare. I unbuttoned my shirt as I watched it slide from her silky pale skin, inch by inch.

It fell away from her breasts. She wore nothing beneath it. I took off my sunglasses and dropped them on top of my clothes, my eyes on her nipples, watching them harden in the cool air of the room. The dress caught on her full hips until Sera hooked her thumbs inside and forced it down over her curves, revealing her soft stomach and the dark curls that covered her pussy. She let it go and it pooled around her feet.

Completely naked except for her high-heeled shoes, she stepped out of the dress, leaving it lying on the floor.

Jesus fucking Christ.

She stood waiting, the city lights coming through the window behind her. They danced across her pale skin as I shrugged out of my shirt and kicked off my shoes before taking off my socks. My eyes never left her. I couldn't have looked away if I tried.

Wearing only my slacks, I closed the distance between us and took her perfect face in my hands. She stared up at me with eyes full of hunger. But there was also sadness. And it infuriated me to see it. Because I knew what it meant.

She was sad because she still thought she was going to leave me.

Tightening my fingers in her silky hair, I hissed against her lips when her fingertips skimmed down my stomach, the soft touch burning like fire on my sensitive skin. But it was nothing compared to the heat of the fury in my blood.

I turned with her in my arms and sat on the bed, pulling her across my lap face down and spreading my legs wide. One hand was still in her hair, holding her head down. My other hand came down hard on her bare ass.

Sera screeched and tried to get up, but I threw one of my legs over hers. There was nowhere for her to go. Again, I brought my hand down on her ass.

"What the fuck are you doing?" she yelled.

"You disobeyed me," I told her. *And you're still going to try to leave me.*

"You can't spank me like a child!"

I rubbed her pink skin, feeling the heat from my hand, before I squeezed one luscious cheek. "No," I told her. "I'll spank you like the woman who doesn't have enough sense in her fucking head to keep herself safe." I raised my hand and brought it down, moaning when she jerked on my lap and cried out with the pain. "I'll spank you like the woman who is so fucking foolish she thinks she's going to leave me."

"Enzo—" Her voice turned pleading.

I brought my hand down again, twice fast.

She tried to twist off my lap. "I hate you!"

Sliding two fingers down between her ass cheeks to her pussy, I moaned again. "You're so fucking wet, Sera." I pushed them inside of her, twisting my hand one way and then the other because she was so fucking tight. "I don't think you hate me."

"I do!"

I pumped my fingers in and out of her until she was pressing her ass back to meet them. Then I pulled them out and inserted one into her tight ass. "Fuck..." The word came out on a groan. "Tell me you don't hate me." Keeping one finger in her ass, I pressed my thumb into her pussy. "Tell me," I ordered.

She cried out into the mattress, but wouldn't say it.

Removing my fingers, I slapped her ass hard. "Tell me."

"Fuck you!"

Grabbing her around the waist, I tossed her higher onto the mattress as I got out from under her and shoved down my slacks and my boxer briefs. She flipped over onto her back as I crawled over her. "Tell me," I begged her. "Tell me you don't hate me."

Sera stilled as her eyes met mine. Slowly, her hands came up to cup my face. Her bottom lip quivered. "I don't hate you," she said quietly.

"Thank you," I whispered. Hooking one arm under her leg, I opened her legs wider and slid inside of her as I softly kissed her swollen lips, both of our breaths catching as her body tightened around my cock. I laid still as I kissed her until she started to move restlessly beneath me. Only then did I pull out and thrust back in, my entire body shuddering because she felt so fucking good.

Kissing my way down her neck and chest, I took her nipple in my mouth. Sera arched beneath me, her hips moving and her hands in my hair. But instead of giving in to what she wanted, I pulled out of her and moved to her other breast before moving down her belly, drawn by the sweet musky scent of her.

I worshipped her body with my mouth, trying to say with sex what I couldn't say with words, making her orgasm with my fingers and my tongue until there was no part of her I hadn't touched. Hadn't tasted. Then, and only then, did I allow myself to bury my cock into her tight pussy, fucking her slowly at first, until my own orgasm slid down my spine and I couldn't hold back anymore. Rising up onto my knees, I pulled her hips onto my lap and fucked her hard and fast, my thumb on her clit so she came with me, pulsing around my cock until I cried out and my eyes rolled back in my fucking head.

When there was nothing left in me, I gazed down at Sera, touching her everywhere I could reach as we both caught our breath. Her eyes met mine, and there was a finality there that made my heart stutter in my chest. She blinked, and it was gone, leaving me to wonder if it was ever there at all. A small smile flirted around her lips.

Carefully, I pulled out of her and laid down behind her. Tomorrow we would talk, and I'd convince her to stay. Her life would be different with me than it was with her father. I'd make her see that it would be, and she would tell me she was going to stay...

Or I'd fucking handcuff her to me until she gave up trying to run. Either way, she wasn't going anywhere ever again.

CHAPTER 17

Serafina

I had to go. I had to go *now*.

I'd woken up to the sound of Enzo's heavy breathing beside me. He'd rolled over and was lying on his stomach, his head turned away from me. The arm closest to me was bent at an angle, his fingers tangled up in my hair.

Slowly and carefully, I extracted the strands from his grip. I waited a few seconds, then began to ease myself off the bed. Muscles I didn't even know I had ached from the best kind of misuse as I crept silently across the floor on bare feet. The dress I'd borrowed laid in a puddle on the floor where I'd left it, and now I stepped into it and pulled it up and on, wincing slightly as the material abraded the tender skin of my ass that was still heated from his large palm.

Tiptoeing back over to the bed, I picked up my shoes and let them dangle from my fingers as I snuck out of the room. In the bedroom doorway, I hesitated. There was a gaping hole in my chest that was making it hard for me to breathe, and it only grew larger the farther I walked away from him. But I told myself not to look back. The man in that bed represented everything I wanted to escape. I didn't want this life of constantly looking over your shoulder, wondering if the person you loved would come home that night or if you'd be visiting them in jail. Or worse—the cemetery.

I wanted to be free. Free to live where I wanted. To do what I wanted. To marry who I wanted. Someone I chose, not a man who took all my choices away from me.

As my eyes roamed down Enzo's muscular back until the sheet blocked my view from the rest of him, I wondered if we'd met under different circumstances...

No. It was best not to go there.

With a new sense of determination, I ignored the ache in my chest and crept through the sitting area to the door that would take me out of there. I had no idea what time it was, but it was still dark, only the city lights coming in through the big windows lighting my way. I shrugged into my jacket and picked up my clutch. I left the wig where it was. Maybe it would be a better idea to take it to disguise my hair, but for some reason I couldn't bring myself to touch it.

As quietly as I could, I turned the deadbolt and unlocked the door. Now all I had to do was open it and walk out.

Instead, I stood there staring at the door as the two warring sides within me battled it out. I knew I needed to leave. Staying in a relationship with Enzo would be toxic and unhealthy. And yet...I didn't want to go. But in the end, my head won over my heart, and, with a shaky hand, I reached for the door handle.

The tips of my fingers had barely touched the cold metal when all of the hair suddenly stood up on the back of my neck. I froze as I heard the sound of a 9mm chambering a round.

"Where do you think you're going, Sera?"

My fingers fell away from the knob, but I didn't turn around. However, I couldn't keep the sorrow from my voice when I answered, "I'm leaving, Enzo."

He made a clicking sound with his tongue. "Are you, though?"

I still didn't turn. I couldn't. I couldn't make myself look at him because I knew what I would see. I could hear it in his voice. The rage. The betrayal. And I didn't think I'd be able to stay strong enough to go if I saw him breaking.

"Step away from the door, Sera."

"Enzo, please," I whispered. "I have to go."

"No, you don't."

I closed my eyes at the razor-sharp pain in his voice. It shredded my heart and left me bleeding, but I had to do this. *I had to.* Because if I didn't pull away from him now, I never would. I put my hand back on the knob.

"Sera."

"I have to," I cried. My fingers tightened on the metal, but I made no move to open the door. I just stood there, waiting for him to either tell me to go or put a bullet in my head.

When he spoke again, he was so close I could feel his warm breath on the back of my neck. "No. You don't." A sob escaped me when I felt the touch of his lips on my bare skin. "You don't have to go anywhere, baby girl. You can stay here with me. Now step away from the fucking door." His arm came around my waist and his free hand covered mine on the door handle. The scent of a dark forest hovered in the air around me, and I breathed in deep, even as my body stiffened.

I tightened my hold and took a small step closer to the door, but he pried my fingers away as he pulled me against his hard body, still warm from the bed. I felt the heat of his skin seep through my jacket and dress, and felt the cold metal of his gun digging into my ribcage.

He pulled me away from the door with him, walking us backward into the hotel room. I could feel his erection pressing into my lower back. The chase excited him. But what would he do when he had me? Would he be content with that?

When we reached the center of the room, he let me go. "Turn around."

Lifting my chin high, I did as he asked. But I would *not* cower before him. I absolutely fucking refused.

Enzo

I stared down into her beautiful blue-gray eyes and watched as the light within them flickered and dimmed. "No," I told her. "Don't do this, Sera."

"I have to," she told me as tears filled her eyes and spilled down her cheeks. She didn't try to wipe them away, her attention completely focused on me. "Please understand, Enzo."

But I didn't understand. I'd never fucking understand. I staggered back a few steps, tugging at my hair with both hands, but somehow managing not to knock myself in the head with the gun.

I could be a bigger man here and just let her fucking leave. Give her the money in my safe that she'd worked so hard to save up and let her go. I could do what I told her I would do. She could start a new life far away from the mafia and everyone in it. She'd have a new identity, and no one would ever find her, even if anyone cared enough to try. As long as she kept her mouth shut, no one would ever know she was a runaway mafia princess.

And that meant I would have to stay away.

I pressed my palm flat to the center of my chest as I fought to breathe. My heart was racing, and I felt a bead of sweat trickle down my temple.

I started to pace, my eyes swinging wildly around the room as I tried to ground myself.

Three things I can see.

Three things I can hear.

Three things I can feel.

That was easy.

Sera. Sera. Sera. She was everywhere.

Her eyes dropped to my cock and balls, swinging freely between my legs, and her tongue wet her bottom lip before her eyes flew back to my face.

Jesus. I couldn't think when she looked at me like that. I stopped pacing and held my hand out in front of me. "Just...just stay right there. For one second." Walking into the bedroom, I grabbed my boxer briefs and pulled them on.

When I returned, I was relieved to see Sera was still there, right where I'd left her. She'd finger brushed her hair and tucked it behind her ears. It clashed with the red of the dress, and her face was red and puffy from crying, but to me, she'd never looked more beautiful. The only thing missing was the silver hoop that normally adorned her nose.

I threw my arms wide. "What do I have to do?"

Her forehead creased. "Enzo..."

I let my arms fall back to my sides. I still held the gun, but I was afraid to put it down. Afraid she would turn around and walk out that goddamn door if I did. "Tell me what I have to do to keep you. And I'll do it."

She stilled. "There's nothing you can do. I don't want this life. You know that."

Frustration gnawed at my insides. "What you're asking..." My hands clenched into fists and released again. "I'd never fit in anywhere else. Not in the normal world. I couldn't live like that."

"And I can't live in this one."

"Not even if it has me in it?"

For a moment, she didn't respond. She just looked at me with her bright eyes, glassy with more unshed tears. "I'm not asking anything of you. Except to let me leave."

I shook my head. "No." She was fucking killing me here. Putting me in a position that I swore I'd never find myself in again. And there was only one thing I could do.

I had to make a choice.

And right now, with her scent on my skin and her perfect face so twisted with pain—the same pain that was eating me alive inside—the answer was standing right in front of me. Tension pulsed between us. The same energy that was always there. It poked and prodded at the shell I'd built around my heart, searching for a way in. "I need to ask you something, Sera."

Her eyes searched my face.

"Do you really *want* to leave me?" My heart sped up as I waited for her answer. "If tonight hadn't happened, if we hadn't met the way we had, would you still want to be free? Of me?"

She started to respond, then stopped. I wanted to go to her. To throw her over my shoulder and take her back to the bedroom and tie her to the fucking bed. But I forced myself to be still as I fought down a new wave of panic that was trying to rise inside of me. "Honestly?" she asked.

I gave her a nod.

"No," she said quietly. The tears that had been gathering in the corners of her blue-gray eyes spilled over. "And I'm probably the sorriest excuse for women's rights in the entire universe, but even after everything you've done to me... No, Enzo, I don't want to leave you."

Relief flooded my veins, so fast and hard I swayed on my feet. And not even her next words could distinguish it.

"But I can't stay here, Enzo. I don't want to live my life like this."

I stared down at this woman who had taken my world and upended it with nothing but her gapped-tooth smile, and the words were coming out of my mouth before I could stop them. "You don't have to." I expected it to be hard to say. Thought the words would get stuck in my throat. I was wrong. "You don't have to," I repeated. "Give me a few minutes to get cleaned up, and then I'll just have to stop at Luca's and let him and Tristan know what's going on."

She looked at me like I'd just grown two heads. "What are you saying?"

"After I talk to Luca, we can go anywhere you want to go."

"Enzo, what are you saying?" she repeated louder.

"I'm saying if you won't stay in my world, then I will go into yours. I have enough money that we won't want for anything for a long time. We'll go wherever you want to. We can move to Mexico. Alaska. Europe...whatever you want."

"But what about your family here? The people you swore you would never leave?"

I didn't know. I didn't know how hard or easy it would be to leave the mafia. There were those who would think I was a rat, and that's why I'd run away. Others maybe wouldn't be satisfied with letting me out. We would have to stay on the move.

Luca, though, he would let me go. Because he loved me as I loved him and he'd want me to be happy. Unable to stand the distance between us anymore, I strode up to her and took her face in my hands, careful not to hurt her as I still held my gun. "*You* are the only light in my life, Sera. I can't let you walk out of it and leave me in the darkness." Gently, I stroked my thumbs along her cheekbones. "I made the wrong choice before. I won't make the wrong choice again."

She wrapped her hands around my wrists, but didn't try to pull me away. "I can't ask you to do this."

"You didn't ask. If this is the only way to be with you, then this is what I'll do." I stared down into her eyes. Those beautiful eyes that swallowed my soul until it was a part of her. "Marry me."

The way she looked at me made me wonder if what I heard in my head and what I'd said were two different things.

"What?"

"Marry me, Sera."

A nervous laugh burst from her. "I can't marry you."

"Why not?"

"Because..." she trailed off.

"That's not a good enough reason."

She gave me a look like I'd lost my mind and took a few steps back until she was out of my reach and I was forced to let her go. Then she walked around me to stand by the windows.

I followed her, but gave her her space and allowed her to think it through for a few minutes. When she faced me again, I knew by the look on her face she was going to refuse me again. "Enzo, we barely know each other."

"You know me, Sera."

She was surprised by my answer, but only for a moment. "You're right. I do know you. You're a mafia man. And you always will be. You'll never be able to escape it. And neither will I if I stay with you. It won't matter where we go, or how fast we run."

"That's not all I am," I told her. "I'm also just a man. A man who doesn't want to lose you."

She opened her mouth. Closed it. "Enzo, this is crazy."

"Why?" And in that moment, it didn't seem crazy at all. It was the most natural thing in the world, and I couldn't for the life of me remember why I'd been fighting so hard against it. Sera wasn't Alessandra. She'd grown up in this world. She knew who I was. She would be a good wife. It would work. We would make it work. "You said you wanted to be with me."

"I do."

I reached for her hand. "Then do me the *honor* of being my wife, Sera. Stay with me."

At first, I thought she was finally going to relent. Her eyes softened, and a smile played around the corners of her mouth. Reaching up with her free hand, she touched my face. Just a brush of her fingertips before I leaned down and took her lips with mine.

Her bottom lip trembled beneath mine as she pulled away just far enough that I could see her eyes. See that she meant what she said.

"I'm sorry, Enzo. I can't."

CHAPTER 18

Serafina

Watching him, I saw the exact moment when he understood that I wasn't going to change my mind. And that he couldn't make me.

And yet, he would try.

His upper lip lifted in a snarl. "Get on your knees."

I kept my eyes on his. He had such beautiful dark eyes. You could see everything in those eyes. Every thought. Every feeling. All the way down to the deepest recesses of his fucked up soul if you looked hard enough. And right now, beneath all this bravado and intensity, he was terrified. I shook my head. "No."

He pressed the muzzle of the gun against my temple. "Get on your *fucking* knees, Sera."

When I didn't immediately obey him, he pressed it harder into my skull, making me wince. I wondered how far I could push him before he'd snap. "You won't do it."

A terrifying smile played around the corners of his mouth as he cocked his head to the side, but he said nothing. However, he didn't need to. I could see everything he was thinking in his eyes. And maybe this was not the night to press my luck. It seemed I'd pushed him enough.

Clenching my jaw, I dropped to my knees. But still, I kept my eyes on his.

The gun at my temple, he shoved down the front of his boxer briefs and gripped his swollen cock with his free hand. He loved these fucking power games, and I didn't want to feed his obsession, but I couldn't keep my eyes from his body. His sharp jawline and lean neck. The wide shoulders and muscular pecs, the left side decorated with a round tribal tattoo that joined the half-sleeve on his left shoulder and bicep.

I took in his cut abs, strong forearms, and that sexy as fuck "V" that led my eyes right to the prize. His cock jutted straight out between his hips, long and thick and so swollen the head was tinged purple.

Siamo liberi. Liberi di ricominciare. We are free. Free to start over.

The words ran along the front of his right hip, lyrics from a song by Vasco Rossi. I knew them well. Roughly translated...

We are free. Free to fly.
We are free. Free to make mistakes.
We are free. Free to dream.
We are free. Free to start over.

How I WISHED it were true, and that Enzo and I could start over in another time in another world.

"Sera."

The way he said my name, so full of raw need, had chills chasing each other up and down my spine. I knew what he wanted. He'd done this very thing back in the beginning of us. And I would give him this as a parting gift. Something to remember me by.

I placed my hands on his hard thighs. Just that simple touch made him hiss out a breath, and it suddenly occurred to me...

He could hold a gun to my head, make me do whatever fucked up things he wanted, but *I* was the one with the power here.

Me.

Not him.

His cock bobbed in front of my face, a drop of come wetting the tip. My mouth began to water. But still, I held back.

"Put it in your mouth," he ordered huskily.

I glared up at him. "No."

His hand released his cock and tangled in my hair. He tugged me closer until the tip of it rubbed the crease of my lips, wetting them. "Suck it. Put my cock in your sweet mouth, or I swear to God and all that is holy, I'll pull this fucking trigger."

He was shaking with the effort it took him to hold himself still. I waited until a low growl raised the hairs on the back of my neck. Then, and only then, did I lick the warm semen from my lips before I parted them for him.

Because I wanted this as much as he did.

Using my hair to guide me, he shoved himself into my mouth, moaning as my teeth scraped along the tender skin of his swollen sex. As soon as he had what he wanted, he dropped the gun on the floor and kicked it out of my reach. Then he held my head with both hands, pulling himself halfway out and then pushing back in. He stayed like that for a few seconds, his eyes staring hungrily at the way my mouth stretched around his girth before he started rocking his hips in a steady rhythm. Rough and deep. Only my hands on his thighs kept him from completely gagging me.

As much as I fought him, a part of me did it because I loved to push him over the edge. I loved the way he wanted me. My name on his lips was spoken with more reverence than the name of a god. And when I sucked him hard and raised my eyes to his, he shouted it for the entire fucking hotel to hear and came in my mouth, hot spurts shooting down my throat. Having no other choice, I swallowed it all, and I moaned for more when he was finished. My skin felt far too sensitive, my panties were soaked, and I could feel my pulse in my clit.

But I needn't have worried. Enzo always took care of me. Always.

Pulling out of my mouth, he grabbed me beneath my arms and lifted me off the floor and into his arms, the strength he had surprising me still. He held my head cupped in one hand, pressing my face to his shoulder as he carried me back to the bed. I could feel his heart racing against mine. Feel the tremors of need run through him. And I wrapped my arms and legs around him and held him tight, unabashedly grinding myself against him, broken sounds of need leaving my throat no matter how quiet I tried to be.

"Shhh...I got you, baby." He set me on the floor and took off my jacket, letting it fall in a heap. Then he stepped back, his eyes running over me hungrily, taking in the red dress all the way down my legs to my bare feet in the borrowed heels, and back to my face.

I reached for him, but he shook his head. "Not yet."

My moan of frustration was cut short when he pushed me back onto the bed, shoved his hands under my skirt and pushed it higher onto my thighs until he could see my bare pussy beneath.

Something shifted in the air, subtle but there. He ran one hand up the inside of my thigh. "Why didn't you wear anything under this tonight?"

I moved restlessly on the bed. "Enzo, please."

"Answer me, Sera."

I stilled when I heard the cold tone of his voice.

"Why didn't you wear anything under this dress?"

His eyes caught and held mine, and I shivered when I saw how cold his face was. I knew what he was thinking, and I wasn't having this ridiculous argument with him. Not now. I sat up and tried to scoot off the bed.

He caught me before I could, pushing me back down onto the mattress. "Why won't you answer me?"

"I'm not doing this with you," I told him. "So, either fuck me or get out of my way."

In the blink of an eye, he had one knee on the bed and his hand around my throat, the other beside my head. His cock hung thick and heavy on my bare thigh. I glared up at him as I tried to suck in air, unable to answer him even if I wanted to. Instead of feeding into his jealousy, I reached for his cock, wrapping my hand around it much in the same way he held my throat. I tightened my fingers around the base, feeling his answering squeeze as he temporarily cut off my airway.

Holding his eyes with mine, I ran my hand up and down his length, feeling him swell inside of my fist. With my free hand, I reached up and touched his face with the tips of my fingers. "Fuck me," I mouthed.

He stared at me long and hard, and I could see him warring with himself. He wanted me with a desperation I never could have imagined. But he also needed to reassure himself that I belonged to him. And only him. With a growl, he shifted his grip on my throat to the back and pulled my mouth up to his. His lips crashed into mine and I felt my teeth cut the inside of my lips. Tasted the salty copper of my blood.

Enzo moaned, running his tongue along the wounds until I opened and allowed him full access to my mouth. As he kissed me, I pumped him faster, working him up until we were both out of breath and the bed trembled beneath me from his efforts to hold his weight off of me.

Releasing him, I grabbed his sides and bent my legs and lifted my hips until I could rub the length of him against my slick core. But it wasn't enough, and a whimper of need escaped me before I could stop it. I shoved at his shoulders, but it was like trying to move a mountain. Still, I persisted.

Enzo broke off our kiss. "If you're trying to tell me no now, it's way too fucking late for that, baby."

"Shut up and roll over," I told him, shoving at his shoulders again. For a moment, I didn't think he would, but then he lowered himself down beside me and rolled onto his back, his legs hanging over the side of the bed.

The thought of escaping was long gone. All I could think about was his mouth on my breasts as his thick cock stretched me wide. But I couldn't do this unless it was my way. My choice. He had to give me this much, at least.

I climbed over him, and his hand went immediately to my hips to position me over his cock.

However, that's not what I wanted. Not yet.

Leaning forward onto my hands, I dangled my breast over his mouth. He took it eagerly between his teeth, biting my nipple and then soothing the bite with his warm tongue as both hands came up to cup my breasts. He flicked my hardened nipple, then sucked it into his mouth before switching to the other side.

My eyes closed and my breath came out in gasps as liquid fire shot through my veins straight down to my pussy. I squeezed my thighs together, desperate to ease the ache between them, but my knees were on either side of his body and I couldn't get the friction I wanted.

But he knew what I needed.

Sliding his hands down my sides, he gripped me tight and lifted me until my pussy was over his mouth. I tried to sit down, but he held me there, hovering above him, as he kissed my inner thighs. First one, then the other.

"Enzo, please," I begged him, even as anger flooded through me. This wasn't the way it was supposed to be. But even with me on top, the balance of power had flipped, and he was once again in control. I fought his hold, trying to lower myself onto his mouth, but he held me there effortlessly until I was soaking wet and nearly sobbing with need.

Then, and only then, did he give me what I wanted. Still holding me above him, he ran his nose between my lips and inhaled deeply, releasing his breath with a growl that told me more than words how much he wanted me. It made me fucking crazy.

He flicked his tongue over my clit, and I jerked and cried out as shots of pleasure burst within me. I bent forward, sinking my fingers into the spikes of his hair and trying to lift his head. He laughed, a dark sound, then lowered me over his mouth, running his tongue back to front before finding my aching clit. He sucked the swollen nub into his mouth, twirling his tongue around it once, twice, before he wrapped his arms around my thighs to hold me in place and settled in.

My hands on my breasts, I ground against his mouth as much as I could, urging him on without shame. Because he never allowed me to have any. Incoherent words spilled from my mouth, begging him not to stop as waves of sharp pleasure rolled through me, building ever higher until they crested, my entire body stiffening at the mixture of pain and pleasure that held it until it released me, pulsing through my body so hard my muscles jerked and I collapsed over his head, unable to hold myself upright.

Still holding me to his mouth, Enzo flipped us both over until I was on my back. Rising over me, he pulled me to the edge of the bed and lined up the head of his cock with my pussy. He surged into me, burying himself in my body. My muscles tightened around him, and if I wasn't as slick as I was, his invasion would've been painful. He rode out the rest of my orgasm, pumping fast and hard until I lost my breath and pleasure rushed through me again.

"Open your eyes."

My eyes flew open at his command, and I cried out when the desperation of his gaze crashed into mine. Without looking away, Enzo came down over me, resting his elbows on either side of my head as he possessed my body like he was terrified I would disappear from beneath him.

But it wasn't only fear. It was something else. Something crazy and raw and intimate. Something eternal. I saw it all in his dark eyes. His possession of me. And I wrapped my arms and legs around him and pulled him to me.

I wasn't his possession.

He was *mine*.

CHAPTER 19

Serafina

We were at an impasse.

"I can't lose you, Sera."

I opened my eyes and looked up at him. Enzo was still above me, and still inside of me, his dark eyes burning into mine. I stared up into his hard, handsome face and felt my soul tear in two.

Leave?

Or Stay?

I could live without him. I could. I would survive. In these last few months before I'd met him, I'd proven to myself that I was able to survive without the help of anyone else. I'd found a job. I'd made a friend. And I'd survived. And I was happy. I was free.

Until the night I'd knocked on this man's door and everything had changed.

"Stay with me." He brushed his lips over mine, and my heart ached at the tenderness in that kiss, so unlike him.

"I can't live my life always running," I told him. "And you can't tell me our life together will be all white picket fences and children and dogs running in the yard. It would be a life on the run. You can't just up and leave the mafia, Enzo."

He rolled off of me, but stayed close, propping his head up on his elbow so he could see my face. "You're right. Between your new reputation and mine, we would always be looking over our shoulder if we were together."

It's the same thing I'd been thinking, but to hear him say it out loud...I choked down the sob in my throat.

"I have an offer for you," he said.

I didn't trust myself to speak yet, so I watched his expression, waiting for him to say more.

"Let's go back to our original deal we agreed on."

"The deal that we've both reneged on?"

One corner of his mouth turned up. "Yes. That one." All amusement left his face. "I swear I'll uphold my end. We'll draw up a contract. Put it in writing with witnesses. All I ask is that you stay with me, without constantly thinking of ways you can escape, for one month. If, after that one month, you still want to go, I'll give you everything I promised for you to start your life over. That will also give us enough time for all this shit around Luigi's death to settle down. Once the capos see you're not a threat, they'll move on to other things to worry about." He brushed a few strands of hair from my face. "But I'm hoping that after that one month, you'll see it won't be so bad for you if you stayed."

I wanted to believe him.

"Give me a chance, Sera. That's all I'm asking for. I just want a fucking chance."

"I find it hard to believe you'll just let me go if that's what I choose."

"And you'd be correct, but that gives me a month to figure out a way for us to have a life together without my family hunting us down."

I smiled, but it quickly faded away. "You told me once that you made a vow to Luca never to leave him. You've spent most of your life protecting him. How will you just be able to leave?" It was a nice fantasy. But I knew mafia men, and I knew this man in particular. I could see how deep his loyalty ran to the two men he considered closer than family.

His dark eyes, so full of pain and promises, traveled over my face. "Losing either of them would tear me up inside. But I would eventually heal enough to keep going if I had you. Losing you," He paused, as though he was having trouble just saying the words. "Losing you would destroy me completely. I'd never recover from such a loss. And I wouldn't want to. I can't lose another part of me, Sera...I can't."

He was talking about his wife and son.

"And that's why I can't just let you walk away from me without knowing where you are and if you're okay. If you're happy. If you're safe. Please, don't ask me to do that."

It wasn't a confession of love, but it was as close as I was going to get.

For now.

"Okay," I told him. "I'll stay. For one month."

He closed his eyes with relief, yet there was still a shadow of disbelief when he opened them again. Cupping my face in his hand, he leaned down and pressed his lips to mine. "Thank you."

I agreed to go back to Luca's, where the security was better, and thirty minutes later, we walked out of the hotel hand in hand. I waited on the sidewalk, shifting my weight from foot to foot in these damn heels, as Enzo let go of my hand and walked over to the valet counter to have them fetch the SUV so he could take us back to the lake house. It was too early in the morning for most people to be out and the streets were empty other than the very occasional car, usually a cop. They were either sleeping or just falling into their beds after a night at the clubs.

Feeling a sense of peace for the first time in a long time, I smiled at the girl who ran past me with Enzo's keys, watching her as she jogged around the corner to go get the SUV. As I turned my head back to Enzo, something caught my attention out of the corner of my eye. It was just a glint of light off of some kind of hard surface, but it was enough to make me turn my head.

A black car was coming toward us with its headlights off. At first, I thought the person driving must've just forgotten to turn them on. It happened a lot in the city because the streets were so lit up anyway. As it reached the hotel, it slowed and the passenger side window rolled down. The man inside was looking straight at Enzo.

From that moment on, everything seemed to happen both in slow motion and crazy fast all at once.

The barrel of a gun slid out the window, and it was pointed at Enzo. My eyes shifted to him, talking to the other valet, and I moved without realizing what I was doing, my mouth open to scream his name.

I watched as his head whipped around, his eyes latching onto me, trying to see what was wrong before the car caught his attention. He threw out his hand—to reach for me? To push me away?—just as I heard the pop of gunshots. Terrified he was going to die right in front of my eyes, I threw myself at him. I think I was trying to knock him out of the way.

Something hit me in the back, right above my left shoulder blade, and again, a little bit lower. The force of the impact threw me against Enzo, but he caught me and lowered me down to the ground. Pain flared through my torso until I gagged on it as I tried to hang onto him. To pull him down with me out of the way.

Black dots danced in front of my eyes. They began to flutter closed, and I fought to keep them open as I watched Enzo. He was crouched over me, one arm around my shoulders and the other hand holding his gun as he fired shots back at the car. I heard a squeal of tires and smelled burning rubber...

The next time I opened my eyes it was to see Enzo's face above mine, his dark eyes searching my face, and I was so happy he took off his sunglasses so I could see his beautiful eyes.

"Sera!"

"SERA!!"

I opened my mouth to ask if he was okay. I tried to tell him that it hurt. That I was sorry. But I couldn't get my voice to work.

And then blackness danced at the corners of my vision, closing in until there was nothing.

CHAPTER 20

Enzo

B lood. There was so much blood.

My cell phone kept slipping out of my hand as I tried to dial 911. Holding Sera up off the ground with one arm, I wiped my other hand on my pants and tried again. This time I got through.

"911. What's your emergency?"

I gave him my location, but not my name. "I have a gunshot victim on the sidewalk in front of the hotel. She was hit twice in the back and she's bleeding profusely and she's unconscious. Please hurry." I ended the call before they could start asking more questions.

The valet pulled up with the SUV, her mouth falling open when she got out, leaving it running for me. I couldn't be here when the ambulance showed up because the police would be hot on their tail. I'd be taken in for questioning, stuck in a goddamn holding room while Sera fought for her life.

That wasn't fucking happening.

"You." I pointed at the girl who still stood next to the SUV with her hands covering her mouth. "Come here."

She shook her head, her eyes about to pop out of her head.

I pulled out my gun and pointed it at her. "I don't have time for this shit. Get the fuck over here. And give me your jacket."

This time, she did as I told her.

"Come around over here and hold her head on your lap up off the ground." I was trying to move Sera as little as possible. "Wad up your coat and hold it over the wounds to try to stop the bleeding."

She looked at the blood. Looked at me. And then back at the blood.

"What's your name?" I asked her.

"Cynthia."

"Cynthia, this is Sera. She's been shot by someone who was aiming for me. I can't stay here with her. Do you understand?"

She nodded.

"You know who I am?"

This time, she made the effort to pull herself together. "Yes."

"Then you know I can't be here when the cops show up. So I need you to stay with Sera. Can you do that?"

"Yes." Ignoring the blood, she pulled off her jacket, kneeled on the pavement, and sat back on her heels as I transferred Sera carefully to her lap. Carefully, I pressed the girl's jacket against the wounds, replacing my hands with hers. Off in the distance, I heard the first sirens.

"What do you tell them when they get here?"

"We were just standing at our station when this lady walked out of the hotel. A car slowed down and shot her. We don't know who she is or who she was with. She's not a registered guest."

"Excellent. Find out what hospital they're taking her to and leave the name at the front desk." I stood up and tucked my gun back into its holster. "You got that?" I asked the guy working with her.

"Yes, sir."

The ambulance was turning the corner as I got into the SUV and pulled away from the hotel. I watched in my rearview mirror as the valet waved his arms and flagged them down, pointing to where Sera lay on the ground.

Turning on the Bluetooth, I called Luca. He answered on the second ring. "What's happened?"

My voice was shaking as I told him what had just gone down.

"Did you get a good look at the shooter?"

"Yes, but most of his face was covered."

"You can't stay in that hotel anymore."

"I know."

"As soon as Sera is stable, we'll have her brought here. I'll call in my doctors."

"Thank you."

"Get back to the house, Enz. And be careful. I'll tell the guards at the house to be on alert, just in case."

He ended the call, and I concentrated on the road. I couldn't get pulled over. I was covered in Sera's blood, and I was on the verge of a panic attack to end all panic attacks. My heart was racing and sweat trickled down my back. I could barely hang onto the steering wheel.

What if she was dead?

I gave my head a good shake. She wasn't dead. She couldn't be dead.

I slammed my fist down on the wheel over and over. If she was gone, it was my own fault. I'd let my guard down. Just for one fucking minute.

It was my fault.

No. No. She wasn't dead. She couldn't be dead. As soon as I got to Luca's, I'd call the hotel and get the name of the hospital she'd been taken to. She would live. If I had to kill every other patient in that fucking place to make sure she got the help she needed, I would.

I drove carefully all the way to the lake house, mostly on autopilot. When I arrived, the guards at the gate were watching for me, guns at the ready. I couldn't even tell them if I'd been followed or not. As soon as I got inside the gates, I let go of the tight control I'd been hanging onto for the last forty minutes. Punching my foot down on the gas pedal, I flew the rest of the way to the house and skidded to a stop right outside the front door.

Luca, Tristan, and even Veda were there when I fell out of the SUV. Luca caught me in his arms before I could fall to my knees, and Veda quickly ducked under my other arm and helped him take me into the house while Tristan took the SUV to the garage. It would need to be thoroughly cleaned to remove all of the blood.

"She's dead," I told them.

"She's not dead," Veda insisted. "What hospital did they take her to?"

"I don't know. I have to call the hotel."

They got me to the couch in the sitting area by the patio doors that led to the pool. I gazed out at the rippling water, seeing Sera as I stared out at the sunset.

"Enzo."

Luca's voice penetrated through the ringing in my ears.

"Call the hotel."

Yes. I needed to find out what hospital Sera was in. I fumbled with my phone again as I pulled it out of my pocket and dialed the hotel's phone number I knew by heart. The desk clerk picked up right away. "The girl who was shot," I told her. "Where did they take her?"

She gave me the name of the hospital where the EMTs said they were taking Sera.

"I'll be sending someone to get my things from my room there. Once it's empty, I'll notify you. I'll also leave a very large tip for your trouble. Thank you." As soon as I ended the call, I told Luca and Veda where Sera was taken.

"I'll call and see what I can find out," Veda told me. With a reassuring smile, she ran up to their bedroom to get her phone.

Luca and I waited in silence to see what she could find out. It didn't take her long.

"She's alive," she called from the landing at the top of the stairs. "She's in surgery."

"See, my friend? She's going to be all right." Luca put his hand on my knee.

"I need to be there."

"You can't Enzo. Whoever took a shot at you will be waiting. They'll be expecting you to show up at the hospital eventually. It's safer for you, and for Sera, if you stay here. We'll go get her as soon as we're able."

I knew he was right. But I couldn't just sit here. Restless, I got up from the couch and began to pace back and forth.

Luca stayed with me until Sera was out of surgery and stable. And then he sent his doctors to go get her. She was being transferred.

SERA WAS KEPT SEDATED for the first few days after she arrived at Luca's. She'd suffered a collapsed lung during the trip, but otherwise had relatively minor injuries, all things considered. The first bullet had gone straight through her shoulder. The second they had to remove at the hospital. It had also torn through her small intestine, but the doctors were able to patch her up. She'd lost a lot of blood, but somehow, she'd made it through.

I had her put upstairs in our bed, and during that time, I never left her side except to shower and use the bathroom. Lisa or Veda brought food up for me. And on occasion, Luca or Tristan would stop in and give me updates on what they'd found out about the shooters. Unfortunately, it wasn't much. No one had gotten a plate number from the vehicle, and since the shooter had most of his face covered, I wasn't able to recognize him. But I wasn't concerned. The truth would come out sooner or later. It always did.

I'd pulled one of the chairs from over by the window to the bed, and that was where I spent most of my time when I wasn't sleeping beside her. So that's where I was when I heard her voice, raspy from disuse, for the first time in way too long.

"Hey."

I lifted my head and my eyes clashed with Sera's. The light inside of them was a bit dull, but it was there. "Hey," I told her softly. Relief washed over me in such a strong wave, I felt a little lightheaded. "You're back."

She looked past me and then around that room. "I'm in our room."

"We had you transferred from the hospital. Luca has a team of doctors who come by every few hours to check you. One of them stays here at the house at all times in case of an emergency. You're in good hands."

Her eyes came back to my face. "You look like hell."

I smiled. "You look beautiful."

"Am I going to be okay?"

"Do you think I would let a couple of gunshots take you away from me after I've fought so hard to keep you here?"

She smiled. "I guess not."

I narrowed my eyes at her. "However, we're going to have a talk about this shit you pulled. What the fuck were you thinking, Sera?"

She reached across the bed and took my hand. "I was thinking that I couldn't just stand there and watch you die right in front of me."

"So you decided to throw yourself in front of a bullet?"

"No. I was just trying to push you out of the way."

I took her hand in both of mine and leaned closer, sticking my face in hers. "You could've been fucking killed," I snarled.

She squeezed my fingers. "That wasn't my intention."

"I don't need you to protect me," I told her. "Do you understand? Don't you ever, EVER, pull that kind of shit again."

A small smile broke out on her perfect face as I yelled at her.

"Jesus Christ, Sera." I pulled her hand to my mouth and kissed her fingers. "Promise me you'll never do anything so stupid again. You can't put yourself in danger like that. My heart can't take it."

"I promise I'll try."

"Marry me," I begged. "Marry me and let me keep you safe."

She didn't refuse me right away this time. "Why do you always insist on proposing to me when I look like shit?"

"You're beautiful," I told her again, and I meant it. "I've never met anyone as beautiful as you."

She laughed, touching her hair self-consciously. "You're lying."

"I'm not." I wracked my brain, trying to think of something I could say that would convince her to bind herself to me. Forever. "Please, marry me." I shook my head before she could say anything else. "Don't," I told her. "Don't refuse me again."

"Is that an order?"

"No. It's a plea. Sera..." I took a deep breath. I wasn't good with words. They made me feel exposed. Vulnerable. But I knew they needed to be said. And maybe, over time, it would get easier to say them. "I love you. And I really wish you would just...fucking *let* me."

She stared up at me, her blue-gray eyes too big for her face. "Okay," she said softly.

It took me a moment to comprehend her answer. "Okay?"

She nodded her head, and a gorgeous fucking smile broke out across her face. "Yes. Okay." She suddenly got serious. "When I saw that gun aimed at you..." Her voice broke, and she cleared her throat. "I just...I couldn't..." She looked away, but I didn't miss the tears filling her eyes.

"Hey, hey. None of that, baby girl. I'm right here, thanks to you. And I'm not going anywhere."

She wiped at her face with her free hand and then turned back to look at me. "But you can't lock me up in the bedroom."

"I can't promise you that," I told her honestly.

She smiled, and I leaned over and took her mouth with mine in a possessive kiss.

My *wife*.

EPILOGUE

Tristan

"Are you ready?"

I looked over my shoulder to find Enzo standing in the doorway to my room, dressed all in black except for the white flower pinned to his lapel. I didn't miss the way his eyes flickered over the scars on my back. He was good at hiding his shock from me. Always had been. Much more so than Luca the few times he'd seen me without a shirt. Or perhaps he was just used to the pieces of torn up flesh that had never had the chance to heal correctly.

I didn't turn toward him as I picked up my dress shirt from the bed and shrugged it on. The front of me was much worse. "Coming," I told him.

He leaned against the doorjamb with his big arms crossed over his chest. But he wasn't fooling me. I could see the way his hands shook because he was holding his sunglasses dangling from the fingers of one hand.

"Are you all right?" Finished buttoning my shirt, I picked up my black jacket and faced him. "If you want to make a run for it, I'll drive."

One side of his mouth turned up in a partial grin, but his eyes couldn't hide his distress. "More like I'm terrified Sera will be the one who runs while we're all distracted, and she'll leave me standing there at the altar like an *idiota*."

"That's not going to happen," I reassured him.

"How do you know?"

"Because Luca posted extra guards."

For a moment, he looked at me like he didn't quite believe me. And then a real smile broke out across his face. "Remind me to thank him later."

I joined him at the door. "Come on, let's go before your bride finds a way to get past them."

Enzo slid on his sunglasses and moved out of the way so we could head downstairs and outside. They were having their wedding on Luca's back deck, which had been decorated for the occasion with flowers and candles. Luckily, the weather was on our side, and it was actually going to be a nice day for January. Not too hot, not too cold, and sunny.

Enzo had insisted on the ceremony taking place at sunset, because that was Sera's favorite time of day. They would say their vows as the sky turned colors behind them.

If I could feel anything at all, I might think that was sweet.

Only a few select guests had been invited. Those who now knew Luca's location out of necessity. I didn't like it. It made me nervous. But as Luca was the boss now, the capos needed to have access to him. They were already seated around the pool when we came out. Sera's father, Ciro, on one side with a few of his men, and Gino and a few others on the other side where Luca and Veda sat. Sera did not want her father to walk her down the aisle. She was going to make the trip alone. Something about how it signified that this marriage was her choice. She hadn't wanted him there at all, but she understood that it was better to keep the peace.

Ciro wasn't happy when he heard about Luigi's death. Apparently, Luca's father had offered to pay quite a large sum of money for the honor of his daughter to abuse in whatever ways he desired, and he hadn't received it all yet. However, Enzo had offered to pay him the remaining sum of money to take her off his hands. And Ciro, knowing he wasn't really being given a choice, agreed.

I took my place at the back of the crowd as Enzo walked up to the railing where the justice of the peace waited to start the ceremony. He smiled at Enzo, and then they both looked toward the patio doors where Sera would be coming out.

As we waited for the bride, I scanned the guests and noticed someone new sitting beside Gino. A woman with long, straight dark hair, her shoulders covered in a cream-colored fur. That was all I could see of her from where I stood. As I watched, he said something to her and laughed, but she didn't laugh with him. Instead, she stiffened and continued to stare straight ahead.

My attention was temporarily diverted by the sight of Sera walking out onto the deck. I had to admit, she was a very pretty woman, even with her pink hair. She wore it with the front pulled away from her face and the rest hanging down her back. Nothing covered it. The dress she wore was off the shoulder, all lace and embroidery on top and a full, fluffy skirt. I had no idea what kind of material it was, but she looked like a princess with her bouquet of purple and white wildflowers.

She was also nervous. Her back was too straight, and her chin was lifted as she caught sight of Enzo and started to make her way toward him to the accompaniment of the classical music playing softly through the outdoor speakers. I watched the guests as they stood up, especially her father. He didn't look happy, but he stayed by his seat at least and didn't cause a scene.

Enzo reached for her hand when she got close to him and as soon as she took it, much of the tension left her shoulders. Sera smiled at him, and my friend only had eyes for his bride. They never took their eyes from one another as everyone took their seats and the JP began the ceremony.

Once I knew no one was going to make an ass of themselves, my eyes went back to the dark-haired girl where she stood by Gino. She was tall, easily almost my height, and it made me wonder if she had heels on or if she was really that height. Her long hair hung halfway down her back in thick, black waves. Her hands stayed clasped in front of her, and she didn't watch the bride with everyone else. I couldn't say why, but she felt familiar to me. Yet I knew I'd never met her before tonight. This was the first time he'd shown up with her on his arm.

I watched her throughout the entire ceremony, and she never once turned her head or looked anywhere other than straight ahead until the vows had been spoken and Enzo kissed his bride to the applause of all who were watching. Everyone stood again as the newly married pair made their way around the pool and into the house where there would be drinks and hors d'oeuvres while the chairs were broken down and the band Luca and Veda had hired set up in the covered sitting area next to the pool.

As the guests began to follow the happy couple, I stayed where I was beside the patio doors. I don't know why there was this need inside of me to see her face, just once, but I couldn't shake it.

And so, I waited.

Gino and his date walked behind Ciro and his men, and all I could see of her was the top of her head over a pair of broad shoulders. She kept her head down as she walked with Ciro's arm around her waist. Distractedly, I wondered why she was wearing a fur when the weather was so nice, although it was supposed to cool down after dark, so perhaps that was it.

Ciro passed me with barely a glance, and then it was Gino and the woman. I could see the pale ivory skin of her face clearly now. The dark slashes of her eyebrows, her delicate cheekbones, and perfectly full lips. But still, she kept her eyes down.

Look at me.

Almost as if she heard me, she looked up and her eyes clashed directly with mine. I watched them widen, almost in fear, before she quickly lowered them again. But not before I saw the clear cobalt blue of her irises framed by long, black lashes.

"Who is that woman?" I asked Luca when he and Veda stopped alongside me. "The one with Gino."

"I heard she was payment for a gambling debt that was owed to him," he told me. Veda looked at the woman with new interest, and I could tell that she was disturbed by his answer.

However, things like this happened all the time. It never bothered me before. It wasn't my business. So why was it, with this woman, I suddenly wanted to *make* it my business?

"Tris? What is it?"

Tearing my eyes away from the woman's long, bare legs—that I could now clearly see across the room, along with the four-inch black heels she was wearing with her red dress—I turned back to Luca. "I just feel like I know her from somewhere."

"I would forget about her if I were you," Luca warned. "She's Gino's property now. And you know how he gets. I don't want to rock the boat with him right now."

I nodded in agreement. I didn't want to rock the boat either.

I wanted to fucking sink it.

Thank you so much for reading Enzo and Sera's story! I hope you enjoyed it. And don't worry, I haven't forgotten about Tristan! His story is coming soon!

If you haven't read Luca and Veda's story yet, you can find it here:

Click HERE to read His Game,
book 1 of His Obsession Trilogy

Or keep going to see the entire list of available books!

To stay up to date with new releases and book
availability, sign up for my newsletter HERE.

ABOUT THE AUTHOR

Hi! My name is Angel Rayne and I write dark, delicious romance with antiheroes who would burn down the world to save the woman they love. I never understood why the villains never win the girl, and so I decided to write them their own love stories where they do.

Here are a few other odds and ends about me...

-Music inspires my stories and I make playlists for every book.

-I am not a fast writer. My stories take time to write. They need to brew in my head. To have book releases close together I have to write ahead. But I would much rather take the time the stories need to be the best they can be than try to rush them out. Trust me on this one.

-I love the rain, and I'm happiest when I'm sitting in a coffee shop with my laptop as it storms outside.

-I prefer to go watch movies alone, with one of those fancy coffees hidden in my purse. (Yes, I really do this.)

-My husband calls me his "little bird" because anything that sparkles catches my eye.

-I will never have enough soft blankets. Ever.

-I love ALL THE DRAMA...but only in books.

-I will forever re-watch The Phantom of the Opera with the hope that by some miracle, this time Christine will choose the right guy.

Thank you for reading my stories, and I always love to hear from you! You can reach me at: angel@angelrayne.com

Ingram Content Group UK Ltd.
Milton Keynes UK
UKHW040728260623
424053UK00001B/24

9 781945 499753